CHASING ALEDWEN

FATED SEASONS: SPRING #1

LAURA GREENWOOD

NORTH LINCOLNSHIRE

Cover Design by: Arizona Tape

Visit Laura Greenwood's website at:

www.authorlauragreenwood.co.uk

www.facebook.com/authorlauragreenwood/

To my readers, Skye, Kelly, Gina and Arizona,

Thank you for supporting me when I cocked this one up. For going "we'll help" when it all felt hopeless to me. It means the world to me, and I don't think I can ever properly express my gratitude.

Now enough with the mushy stuff, let's go get Dwen her men.

A NOTE ON LANGUAGE

Please note that the author of this book is from the UK, and as such, spellings and some turns of phrase will appear in British English.

WARNING

Chasing Aledwen is a paranormal reverse harem. There are four love interests, and the heroine doesn't have to choose between them.

BLURB

No one said being a Princess was easy, and for Aledwen, the Fae Princess of Spring, it's even harder. Especially with her lack of magic, and the upcoming Birth of Spring. A ceremony she should be performing for the first time, but can't.

Luckily, she doesn't have to figure it out alone. Though at times, her shifter mates seem to be more of a hindrance than a help. And her elf's sense of duty may just over ride the bond between them.

Can Aledwen become the Queen she was always meant to be? Or will she be stuck as a magicless Princess.

Chasing Aledwen is a RH set in the Paranormal Council Universe, and is the second book in the Fated Seasons series.

ONE

Aledwen studied the ornate staircase with a look of intense distaste on her face. It was too garish, and too gold for her liking, but then she didn't really have much of a choice in the matter. For the moment, this was someone else's palace.

"You'll enter up there, and descend down the stairs, where your mother will meet you," the Master of Ceremonies instructed her. Aledwen grimaced. She didn't like the sound of what he was suggesting at all.

The problem wasn't that she had to do something formal. She was a Princess, she'd been doing these things her entire life, even if her mother did keep her hidden away from everyone else. No, Aledwen's problem was this particular ceremony, otherwise known as the Birth of Spring. Her family had been performing it for millennia, with each Princess taking over from her mother when she reached eighteen. Aka, Aledwen's age.

Which was all very well, but Aledwen's magic didn't work right. Or at all.

"Got it," she muttered to herself. She'd been thinking and dreaming about this day since she was a child. Though the dreams had turned into nightmares more recently. Around the same time she realised her magic wasn't just going to miraculously arrive one day. Not without her doing something to help it. And while she'd scoured the book shelves in the palace library, and some in the local settlement too, she'd yet to find anything that could help her. It was beginning to get highly frustrating to say the least.

"Then you'll walk over to her Majesty the Queen and you'll..."

"Thank you, I know what I need to do," she interrupted, holding up her hand to stop the man from saying the words that would just make everyone in the room awkward. No one needed to remind her she had to take off her robe and...

She didn't want to think about it. Without magic, there'd be nothing to shield her from the Court's gaze. They'd all be able to see just how naked she'd be. Exposed and ready to be ridiculed by them all. She'd love to be able to say none of them would act like that, but what did she know? She wasn't even allowed around people most of the time.

At least with the Birth close, Aledwen was able to spend time actually in her mother's Court, and not just observing in secret. If anyone found out she'd been doing that then there'd be hell to pay, she was sure of that.

From afar, it had always seemed interesting, far more so than the countless balls and parties the other fae seemed to enjoy. She'd far prefer to be embroiled in the politics of the world than to be stuffed into a ball gown. She guessed now she'd be both.

"But, Your Majesty..."

"That's fine, thank you, Carter. I'll be okay from here." She smiled at him to soften the blow, but from the conflicted look on his face, she didn't know whether she'd actually managed. Insulting the palace staff, accidentally or not, wasn't in her daily plan. After all, one day she was going to have to rule here. She didn't want them hating her even before that day came.

She watched him leave, taking the last of the serving staff with him. Good, she was better off alone to coming to terms with what she had to do.

Going back to the start, she serenely walked the path she would for the Birth, conscious that she needed to get it right when the time came. If she was going to end up naked and ridiculed, then she was going to do everything else right before hand. She wasn't going to be known as the fae princess who really messed it up.

"So you're the one they're all talking about." A smooth male voice made her jump out of her skin, and she turned to see a man leaning against the door frame of the room. There was something about it that sent a thrill through Aledwen, even if she knew she shouldn't feel that way.

"Whatever do you mean?" she asked carefully.

"The fae are all talking about you," he replied, completely unhelpfully.

"Do you have a name?" she tried instead.

"Dreyfus, but everyone calls me Drey."

"No wonder," she muttered under her breath. But a low chuckle told her he'd heard. Damn. He probably was something other than a half-fae then. At least for him to be here it meant he was some kind of paranormal. If not then...well she didn't actually know what happened. She knew a lot of human men were brought here for the night. Her father had been one of them. It was just how the fae worked if they never found their fated mate. She hoped she wouldn't end up like that. Kidnapping a human man just to have a child seemed callous at best, down right wrong at worst.

"What do they call you?" he asked, not at all phased by her muttering.

"Dwen."

He raised an eyebrow, and had every right to. Why had she said that? No one had ever called her Dwen. Ever. Not even her mother.

"Aledwen," she corrected herself.

"I think I prefer Dwen. It suits you." He smiled widely, lighting up his face as he pushed away from the door frame and stalked towards her. Despite herself, her traitorous heart fluttered.

"No one calls me Dwen," she stuttered pointlessly.

"Now I can."

"Who are you?"

"Drey."

"Not what I meant," she pointed out, trying to use as much of her royal bearing as possible to get him to listen to her, but she was pretty sure it was wasted on him.

"That's not going to work on me," he replied, proving her point. "I'm not the kind of man easily swayed when he's decided on something." The glint in his eye suggested he was on about more than just telling her who he was. She pushed those thoughts aside. She wasn't used to having them, and even if she was, she shouldn't be having them about strangers.

"What are you doing here?" she tried changing tack.

"I wanted to see the girl everyone was talking about. I must say, I'm surprised to find a beautiful woman in her place."

Aledwen's heart fluttered, and she tried to dampen it. She couldn't be having this behaviour, even if no one but her knew about it. Even so, the compliment was doing funny things to her. She'd long since accepted that she wasn't ugly. But she also wasn't stunningly beautiful. Though it hadn't been too hard to accept that once she'd realised fae weren't the ethereal beings from the human's stories. It'd taken her far longer than she'd have liked to come to that conclusion. She'd been a very sheltered child, and it hadn't been until a few years ago that she'd thought about sneaking about and learning more about her people. The *real* side. Not the pretty picture her mother wanted her to know.

It had always baffled Aledwen why her mother wanted to keep her so in the dark. She was the future leader of the Spring Fae, so why wasn't she in the loop about...well, what it was to actually be the leader of them.

"May I have a dance?" the man, Drey, asked suddenly.

"There's no music." She frowned. He'd seemed so normal, if a little intrusive. It wasn't every day that people walked in on her while she was alone. In fact, that never happened. Unless the someone was her mother.

"I've been told I have a good singing voice," he supplied, looking very sure of himself. She was becoming pretty sure of him too, especially how his dark eyes sparkled like gems, and voice flowed through her as sweet as honey.

"I shouldn't dance with you."

He was far too close for her comfort. Or he wasn't. But she *should* have been uncomfortable with it. He was most definitely in her personal space. She also most definitely liked it. He smelled Earthy, and if she had to guess, she'd say he was some kind of shifter. Though she had no real way of knowing for sure. She'd not met a shifter as far as she knew, so would have no idea what one smelled or looked like.

"Why not, Dwen?" His voice was breathy, and she finally began to feel uncomfortable. Though not in the way she should. She'd sneaked out of the palace enough times to have at least some experience in the matter. That didn't mean she was prepared for it though. Especially not from such a large man. She was tall herself, and he wasn't that much taller, but that didn't seem to help. He wasn't even that broad, though he was clearly in good physical shape, but not overly so. Meaning it was something to do with his demeanor as opposed to his actual size.

And she liked it. A lot. But she wasn't ready to let him know that.

"It's not proper." The words slipped out without them intending to, and she slapped her hand over her mouth. She'd sounded like her mother, and that really *wasn't* something she wanted. Her mother lived in the dark ages. It was time to bring the Spring Fae into the light.

Or it would be. If she didn't end up humiliated.

Drey didn't say much, but a knowing smirk crossed over his face, as if he knew what she was thinking about. "Sometimes the best thing to do with proper things is break them."

"I'm sure you're right." She drew herself up to her full height and fixed him a glare. "But that doesn't mean I'm going to give in to you."

Without waiting for him to respond, she pushed past him and stalked from the room.

"I would expect nothing less, princess," he called after her. Aledwen's scowl deepened. He wouldn't be getting his way. No matter what she did, she wouldn't be giving in to him until she was good and ready.

TWO

"That's the elvish ambassador." The Queen's voice was dripping with condescension.

It was a pointless comment anyway. Aledwen *knew* that was the elvish ambassador, because she'd spent her childhood learning to recognise the house crests of all the elvish houses. And he had one blazed across his chest. Paige, if she remembered correctly. And she did. There was no chance she was wrong after all the hours of lessons she'd been given. The white starburst on a green background was pretty iconic too. While some of the houses with the same parents had similar crests, this one was recognisable in its individuality. Mostly because House Paige claimed to be descended from the last elvish kings. Complete rubbish as far as anyone was aware, but they kept trying to make it real anyway.

The man strode towards them, a determined and somber look on his face. "Your Majesties," he said, dipping a shallow bow that barely hinted at respect. If she hadn't been in public, and worried that those privileges would be revoked, she'd have said something about it. But the last thing she wanted to do was end up spending the evening in her room alone again.

The elf stood upright, tall and proud. She could already tell he had a few inches on her. More than Drey had earlier. She ignored thoughts of the other man. He'd been plaguing her mind since she'd left him behind, and she'd more or less decided that if he was at the ball later, then she'd ask him to dance. It was forward of her, there was no denying that. But she hadn't stopped thinking about him since, and it made sense to do something about that.

"What can we do for you, Master Paige?"

Aledwen cringed as her mother's choice of words made the man sneer. Whoever he was, and for whatever unknown reason, he didn't really seem to want to be here. And hated her mother.

"My House sends their regards," he said stiffly.

"And ours, to you," Aledwen replied the formal words she'd been taught as part of her training. His eyes flickered to her, the strange moss green lingering for a moment. He was surprised, she could tell that much, but she wasn't really sure why. She was just being polite even if her mother wasn't.

"They wish to propose a treaty," he said slowly. His gaze slipping to the side to look back at Aledwen. She couldn't help but be a little smug he was doing that. Though maybe it was just curiosity and not knowing who she was. Then again, Drey had known who she was already, and she'd never seen him before. And her long, honey brown hair and oval face were almost an exact replica of her mother's. They barely looked a few years apart in age thanks to fae longevity.

"We have one," her mother said curtly, drawing a horrified look from Aledwen. Surely this wasn't how she should be conducting herself? There was no grace to this. It wasn't how she'd want her court to be run.

"A new one." The man was equally as disdainful of the conversation, which piqued her interest all the more. Something had clearly gone on, whether between the fae and elves as races, or between her mother and the ambassador, Aledwen didn't know. She wasn't sure she wanted to either. There were some things that a daughter really shouldn't know about.

"What's the differences in the treaties?" Aledwen asked softly, mostly so she could beat the Queen to it and actually have a proper conversation with the elf.

"Erh..." The man glanced between the two women, and Aledwen suppressed a smile. He clearly wasn't sure what to make of her interrupting. From her mother's pursed lips, neither was she. But while there was nothing she could do about the past, Aledwen would smooth over whatever she could for the future.

"Well?" she prompted, being sure to keep her voice light and pleasant. Him turning on her like he had her mother wasn't part of her plan. Though using the word plan was a little rich. She was definitely lacking one. Or even the semblance of one. She really should work on that before opening her mouth.

"I don't think here's the place, Your Majesty."

It took Aledwen a moment to remember he was talking to her. Being addressed formally was something she still had to get used to. Most of her servants had known her since she was a child, making it difficult for them to be anything less than slightly over friendly. She didn't mind. She *wanted* to be approachable, and the kind of leader that people were actually comfortable talking to.

"Then why bring it up?" she asked, genuinely curious. If he hadn't wanted to discuss it, then why had he mentioned it in the first place. Her gaze slipped to her mother, who had a slightly alarmed look on her face. Maybe this was out of protocol then? It'd explain why everyone but her sounded surprised.

"I-"

"Never mind," Aledwen interrupted, though she tried to keep her voice as soft as possible. She didn't want him thinking she was rude. Offending another people on her first day at court probably wasn't the best plan. "Why don't we discuss this tomorrow? In the sun room and just after the mid-day meal?"

The man from House Paige nodded, though he seemed a little unsure of the situation still. Good. Putting him on the back foot could be the start of her actually managing to shake things up around here.

"Aledwen," her mother scolded, her eyes boring into her daughter.

"Yes, Your Majesty?" she replied sweetly, knowing that if she used the proper title, it'd rob her mother of any chance to make a scene. Aledwen knew there was a chance her mother might not even try do that, but it was better safe than sorry.

Her mother said nothing. Probably because there wasn't anything for her *to* say, at least not without looking completely unreasonable.

"Don't you need to get ready for the ball this evening?" she asked equally as sweetly. Good. She was rattled then. That would suit Aledwen just fine.

"Yes, mother." She stood up before dipping a brief curtsy. She wouldn't need to start getting ready for another few hours, she wasn't one of those women that needed hours to make sure every tiny hair was in place. But she did know when she was being dismissed.

"Sir," she added, curtsying to the elf too. If he'd been taken aback before, he was even more so now, and she smiled to herself. Satisfied in the reaction she'd caused, she swept out of the room, ignoring the murmurs of the court. What did it matter to her what they thought? None of them knew her, and even if they did, they had no choice in her position. One day she'd be their queen, whether they liked it or not.

THREE

O kay, she'd admit it. She was bored. With the ball too close for her to sneak out of the palace, but far enough away for her to need to do something in between. Except she'd definitely chosen the wrong activity. She should have gone to the archery range and practiced shooting. It'd have occupied her body as well as her brain. Instead, she'd decided to read one of the novels that'd been smuggled in from the human realm. Which had been a really bad decision.

Every time the hero got into a risky situation, she kept picturing Drey in his place. Or occasionally even the ambassador from House Paige. She wasn't sure where *that* one had come from. He'd been pleasant to look at, without a doubt, but he wasn't her type. If she even knew what that was. Reading this book was twisting her up in knots, and she had no idea about how to untangle herself. Or if she even really wanted to. The images were kind of enticing.

"Aledwen?" A voice interrupted her thoughts, and she looked up to see her lady's maid, and close friend, Johanna. She'd been in Aledwen's service since they were both fourteen, and they'd instantly become close. As was to be expected given they'd both led very sheltered upbringings and somewhat boring lives.

"Mmm?" she responded, finally coming out of her daydreams. She shouldn't be thinking about men like that. Her mother would have a fit. Propriety wasn't the only thing she cared about. She was also a staunch believer in the fae women ruling alone. No man by their side to support or do anything for them.

In some respects, Aledwen liked that way of thinking. A woman didn't *need* a man. But that didn't mean she didn't want one. Or two as the case may be. She'd probably read too many of the human novels, but she wanted to be swept off her feet and made to fall in love, just like those heroines were all the time.

A fantasy, true. But what else did she really have to sustain her?

"It's time to get ready," Johanna said, pity filling her eyes. Aledwen grimaced. It'd be fine if the dress she had to wear was pretty. Or fit her well. As it was, she could barely call what she was supposed to put on a dress. Rather, a cake topper or a just a cupcake. That was more like it.

At least it wasn't pink.

Oh wait, it was. Her mother had insisted as it represented the pink cherry blossoms that sprung up everywhere at the beginning of spring. Just about any other colour would have been preferable.

"Very well then." She sighed, setting her book down on the table and stripping herself of the simple dress she'd been wearing today. Yet another out of date tradition the fae seemed to love. No comfortable clothing for them, just old fashioned velvet, satin and cotton. Always stiff from the weird way they had to wash them so they didn't get ruined.

She dropped her dress into the laundry basket, and entered her bathroom. At least this was modern. Sleek marble, hot water, and a tub big enough for ten. Maybe not ten. But probably six. Though she wasn't too sure when she was ever actually going to try that out. It didn't strike her as very princess like behaviour.

Or maybe that was the perfect reason to try it. She smiled to herself as she sunk into the hot water already filling the tub, amused at the idea of how scandalised her mother would be if she ever did that. It would be worth it even for that. She'd soon realise that her little girl wasn't quite the proper lady she wanted her to be.

"Aledwen..." Johanna warned, and she jolted upright in the bath, not realising quite how deep into her fantasy ideas she actually was.

"Sorry, getting out now," she lied, ducking her head under the water, and washing out the imaginary grime. As a fae, there was no need for her to actually wash her hair. It would do it naturally after a bit. But she enjoyed the fragrance that trailed her around after she'd used the apple shampoo she bought from the human shop in the nearby settlement. Oddly, her mother had never asked where she'd gotten it, but that would have meant her paying attention enough to realise something.

She rinsed off, and pushed herself up out of the bath, pulling the plug so it would drain as she did so. She toweled herself off, and hastily dressed in the underwear and slip she'd picked out for the evening. They too were from the human shop. Fae clothing was bad right down to the bottom layer, and she'd long since started buying the softer feeling human stuff. Lucky for her, Johanna completely agreed, and would never betray her trust by revealing she had it.

Pulling the door open, she stepped back into her main room, to find Johanna stood there with a bunch of petticoats in her hands. Reluctantly, Aledwen stepped into them, and waited patiently for Johanna to tie them around her waist. Yet another problem with these outfits. Getting in and out of them alone was virtually impossible.

She grimaced as she realised what was next, but refused to suck in a breath. If there was one thing she definitely had no plans of giving in to, it was having her corset so tight she could barely breathe. Most women did it to attract the visiting male paranormals. Or the half-fae. She likely wouldn't need that even if she was allowed anyway. She was the princess, what man wouldn't want to try and win her. It'd get him imaginary power in most men's eyes.

That done, all she had to do was step into her skirts, which was actually the easiest bit.

Slowly, Johanna ran her hands through Aledwen's hair, drying it with her magic. She really should have been able to do that alone, but without any magic, there wasn't much she could do.

"There." The other woman stood back, admiring her handiwork. "You look beautiful."

"I look like a decoration," Aledwen murmured. Johanna stifled a laugh behind her hand.

"But a beautiful one."

"I'm sure." No one looked good like this. It was royalty goggles all over again. One look at anyone with a title, and a lot of fae got giddy and started rambling on about beauty. Really, fae were just like any other species. There were truly beautiful fae, and not quite so beautiful fae. The only difference was that they often tended to glow. Only faintly, for which Aledwen was glad. Going around with a green filter on everything wasn't exactly her idea of fun. She'd rather experience the world in every colour.

"Thank you," she told Johanna, giving her a weak smile.

"You're welcome." Her friend smiled back, then made a slight shooing motion, indicating that she really should get on her way. She had a ball to get to whether she liked it or not.

The corridor was surprisingly deserted. Everyone must already be in the room preparing to dance the night away. That, or they were drunk down another corridor somewhere. That was how most of the balls she'd been allowed to attend seemed to end up.

Before she knew it, she was at the entrance to the ballroom. And kind of hating that this was the last time she'd be able to enter so unobtrusively. They weren't like the summer court. Balls for the Spring Fae happened rarely, and the next one was in a few days when the Birth would occur. Well, after the Birth. She'd never been allowed to go to that one before, but she'd listened to it every year. Part of her was excited, it was the one party a year where everyone let their hair down. The other part of her was just worried about the bit that came before.

They were worries for another day though. First she had to get through *this* ball and hope that Drey didn't see her in this monstrosity of a dress. Maybe she wouldn't be asking him to dance after all. He'd likely just laugh when he saw her anyway. She would if she were him.

The hall was alive, but everyone was stood the correct distance apart, like propriety dictated. It was odd that they ran the balls and court like they all lived in a nunnery, but sex, alcohol and kidnapping were considered to be just who the fae were. The double standards weren't just baffling, but completely stupid too. It didn't make any sense to Aledwen for them to be that way. She'd rather the fae dropped the kidnapping humans bit, there were enough visiting paranormal men that they really didn't need to do that anymore, but if they wanted to get drunk and have sex, then they should just own it. Preferably not in such uncomfortable dresses though. Maybe that was the point of them. Taking so long to remove it did kind of kill the mood a bit. Unless the man had claws. Then it could be fun.

Her thoughts drifted back to Drey. She wondered what kind of shifter he was. If he even was one, but something in her gut was telling her she was right.

"You summoned, Your Majesty?" The man in question appeared in front of her as if by magic, and gave an exaggerated bow.

"Dreyfus," she acknowledged, cringing inwardly that he was seeing her in such an awful dress. "Would you like to dance?" she asked before he could get in there first. She wanted to be the one in control of the situation, and this seemed to be the best way to achieve that.

"Sure." He smiled easily, not at all put off by her forwardness, which could probably only be a good thing? She wasn't too sure. Maybe that completely counteracted what she was trying to achieve?

He held out his hand, and she took it, tingles running up and down her skin. There was something about him that was calling to her. And not just on the surface either. Something deep down was telling her that she could trust him. That he was on her side. That she was on his. The only thing that was confusing her a little was the lack of urge to drag him into a cupboard and have her way with him. The rest of it sounded like the mating rumours did. But she should want him in *that* way too if it was the case. And while she'd been thinking of it earlier, and found him physically attractive now, she wasn't wanting to quite go that far.

Thinking about it was starting to give her a headache.

"Do you know this song?" he asked casually, and she appreciated his attempt at light conversation.

"Yes, I know most of them. I had dancing tutors as a child." She'd actually enjoyed those lessons. The melody in the music, and the freedom of movement. At least until the corsets had come. Then dancing hadn't been so fun. Quite the opposite. Even as loose as her corset was tonight, there'd likely be bruises come the morning. Not to mention back ache. She could almost feel it already.

He drew her into a firm ballroom hold, and started the intricate steps of the dance. Pleasantly surprised, she followed along with him, giving over to the music. There weren't many men who could dance like this, though that could be because only the half-fae really spent a significant amount of time at court. And even then, they tended to be looked down on as inferior. Another thing she'd change if she could. It wasn't their fault they'd been born male and couldn't inherit the full powers of a fae.

"Where did you learn to dance?" she asked as the music slowed and transitioned into another song. Technically, she believed she was supposed to change partners, but she didn't want to yet. Not when there were so many more dances to enjoy. And questions to be asked. But she hadn't wanted to talk during their first dance for some reason.

"My mother." A haunted look flitted through his dark eyes and she decided to refrain from pushing further. Maybe he'd tell her in time. Wait...in time? What made her think there'd be time? It was the gut feeling she seemed to be having about him again. She should probably just go with it. It'd never served her wrong before.

"Do you enjoy it? Dancing I mean?"

"Yes, it reminds me of her."

They lapsed back into silence, though she was desperate to pry a little more. To learn what made him tick, and to chase away the sadness in his eyes and his voice. The something inside her definitely didn't like the idea of him being hurt.

"Are your parties always this stiff and formal?" he asked after a few more rounds of the dance floor.

"I think so."

"You don't know?" He spun her under his arm, and her dress flared around her. She had to admit that effect was kind of pretty, even if the dress itself was frightfully bad.

"I don't come to many," she admitted, glancing away and pretending to watch the couple in front of them.

"Why not?"

"I just don't."

"What's more your scene then? One of the parties on Earth?" She turned back to him, noting the curious look on his face. He was genuinely interested in her answer it seemed. That was odd to say the least. No one was ever really interested in what she wanted.

"I don't know, I've never been," she answered. This time, his face lit up in response.

"Would you like to?"

She thought for a moment. She'd never been to Earth, and it seemed kind of crazy to agree to go there with someone she'd just met. But on the other hand...

"Yes," she blurted out. "I'd like that very much, thank you."

"Pick you up in an hour?"

"Wait, what?"

"Be ready, Dwen, you have a balcony?" He gave her a cheeky smile, and without realising she was doing it, she nodded along. "Good. I'll meet you there."

"How..."

"Wait and see." He winked at her, before finally breaking their hold and striding off into the crowd. If she was going to escape in an hour, then she really needed to do the rounds so she could sneak away. And hopefully get out of the awful excuse for a dress she was wearing.

FOUR

S he watched as a large shape made its way up to her balcony. She should be nervous, but something was telling her not to be. The same something that was telling her to trust Drey. She guessed that answered what kind of shifter he was. Or it would when he got a little bit closer. Maybe he was a...

No, she couldn't think it. They were far too rare for one of them to have accidentally made their way to her court. And no way would one be heading towards her balcony. The shape drew closer, the huge wingspan dominating the sky.

He was actually a freaking dragon. Of all the things...

Then again, she was a fae princess, and there were only ever four of them in existence at any one time, which might suggest that she was even rarer than a dragon.

She couldn't make out what colour he was from this far away, other than dark. Maybe he'd match his eyes.

She didn't really mind, but just knowing he was a dragon had her head spinning. There were so many questions she needed to ask. Being curious by nature did have its drawbacks, especially for the other people in her life.

He descended towards her balcony, and Aledwen took a step back and away from the edge, knowing she'd be in his way otherwise.

With a surprising amount of grace, he shifted back into human form and landed in a crouch on the tiled floor. His head rose, and his gaze met hers. She was only a little disappointed he was still fully clothed, but at least it meant she could focus and wouldn't end up fixating on bits of him that she shouldn't.

Or should. There was still an odd part of her that was tugging her towards him and telling her that he was a good choice. There was a real possibility she'd give into the urge at some point. It would probably be fun after all.

"You can't wear that," he said by way of greeting.

"I know," she replied. "But I can't take it off on my own."

"What?"

"It's designed for two people to get in and out of. I can't even reach the corset laces at the back." A shiver stole down her spin as she realised how close he'd have to get in order to remove it. Maybe his hands would brush against her skin in the process and...

She couldn't think like this.

"Could you turn around please?" His words sounded laboured, like he was struggling with the same kind of thought that she was. It pleased her to think it, even if it wasn't true.

Slowly, she did as he asked, anticipation building within her. She'd been in this position before, just a couple of times, to try it out when her curiosity had gotten the best of her. But this was different. Something undefined charged the air, and she was excited for what that could mean, even if she didn't dare think it.

He tugged at the laces of her corset, but instead of growing looser, it went the other way, squeezing her chest and making it difficult to breathe. "You might need to be a bit gentler," she gritted out.

"Sorry," he grunted. "I can't seem to work it out."

"You just pull the laces," she pointed out, and felt him try out her request. At least he was willing to listen. That was always a good sign.

"It's not working. How attached are you to this dress?"

"Not at all. Why?" she responded.

She was answered with a sharp ripping sound as the material tore and cold air hit her bare skin. The shiver passing over her had nothing to do with the cold.

The fabric fluttered to the ground, pooling around her feet in a tattered mess. A small smile lifted the side of Aledwen's mouth. That was more like it. The dress was back where it belonged. No one would have to look at it ever again. Other than Johanna if she wasn't back in time to clear it away.

More chill air swirled around her bare skin as she realised he'd ripped through her slip too. Feeling a surprising amount of confidence for the situation, she let that too fall to the floor, and stepped away, turning to face the dragon.

"What should I wear then?" Her voice came out lower than she expected it to. Kind of sultry. And nothing like she'd ever sounded before. Just one of the strange effects the man seemed to be having on her.

"Do you have anything more...form fitting?" He cleared his throat as his eyes trailed up and down her body taking her all in. That put her at the advantage. Why she was so determined to be that, she wasn't all that sure, but the determination was building by the second, and she'd long since learned to listen to her instincts when those things came to pass.

"I think I have something, yes." She smiled to herself as she turned away, but didn't sway her hips as she walked. She was almost certain the game they were playing wasn't one of seduction, and she didn't want to make it one. That would come later. No. As far as Aledwen could tell, this was more a game of control. Not in a negative way though. It felt like more of a game to her than anything. One she could have fun with.

Then they could turn it into a game of seduction. And she'd have great fun doing just that.

Her dressing room was annoyingly far away from the balcony. Apparently the architects hadn't considered someone might end up outside and naked. Though was surprised they'd built a balcony strong enough to support the weight of a dragon shifting. It must have been enchanted at some point, that was the only way she could see it working.

His eyes burned into her back, and she moved extremely carefully as a result, conscious he was constantly watching and appraising her.

She bent over, rummaging around in the back of the dressing room for the package she'd hidden there nearly a year ago. Pulling it out, she shook out the forest green fabric and smiled. *This* dress would be perfect. It was yet another purchase from her human shop, and one of her favourites. Though until now, she hadn't been brave enough to even put it on, not wanting to know what would happen if she was caught in it. Her mother might even have disowned her if she'd discovered it. There was a chance she might not succeed, had she tried. It was virtually impossible to disown a princess unless there was a spare one too.

Luckily, make-up was a human thing, and she had no need of it. Which would save time at least. Though she did think to tie her hair back in a bun. The only way she could think of to sneak out of the palace was going to be on the back of a dragon. Conducive to having her hair whipped around her face, but not so much for anything else. Zipping up the dress was all she needed to feel ready, and once she'd turned around, she nodded to Drey. He smiled and shifted back into his dragon form.

Aledwen approached slowly, not because she was worried about what he'd do to her. More because she was so in awe of the amazing creature in front of her. Logically, she knew it was just Drey, the man she'd danced with just over an hour ago, and the one who made her feel the weird pull towards him. But equally, he was magnificent.

This close up, it became clear that his scales were midnight blue, and they shimmered in the dim light. Slowly, she reached her hand forward and brushed them against the surface. The scales felt like polished glass to touch, smooth and unblemished, with an undeniable warmth beneath them. He wasn't like anything she'd ever touched before, and she imagined she'd never touch anything like him again.

"Wow," she muttered without realising, getting a soft nudge from the dragon's head in response. "Is this okay?" she asked, conscious he may not be used to people touching him, nor wanting them to if they did.

Again, the dragon nodded its head.

"I guess I need to sit on you then?" A blush rose to her cheeks as she realised she'd need to be straddled on top of him for this to work. Exhilaration soon made the uneasiness disperse. She was going to ride on a real life dragon. Not many people would be able to claim that. Not very many ever would. It didn't seem likely that dragons would let a lot of people ride on them.

As carefully as she could, for fear of hurting him, she hoisted herself onto his back and wrapped her arms around his neck, clinging on as tightly as she could. Heights didn't scare her, but the fall from a dragon would certainly land her on the dead side of hurt.

Once she was settled, she felt his wings begin to beat beneath her, the rhythmic movements surprisingly soothing. He lifted into the air, hovering for a few seconds so she could get used to the sensation of the air rushing against her skin.

Then, without waiting a moment longer, he sped off, heading in the direction she knew led to the human realm.

A joy unlike any she'd ever known flowed through her as they flew. No wonder dragons kept this for themselves. If she could fly like this every evening then she would.

A part of her didn't even want to get to Earth, and to the party he'd promised. It wouldn't matter so long as he kept flying her around like this.

FIVE

"Why can't we fly again?" she grumbled as the contraption Drey had called a car rocked from side to side.

"It would raise too many questions if any of the humans suddenly saw a dragon, don't you think?"

"Not the point," she responded instantly, despite knowing that he was likely right. It would likely raise more than a few questions. She just wanted to fly again. But her own wants probably couldn't outweigh the needs of the entire paranormal community. Not if she wanted to retain the little respect she'd actually managed to build as heir to the throne. Which wasn't really much considering she'd only just been introduced to them.

Drey chuckled deeply, making Aledwen pout. She wasn't used to being laughed at, and she hoped he wasn't going to make a habit of it.

"Where are we actually going?" she asked, trying to ignore the annoyance of him laughing.

"The Shifter Council is holding a ball to honour something. Though I'm not sure what. I don't keep up with politics enough." Something dark crossed over his face, and she figured that it was something like guilt causing it. Maybe she'd have time to get it out of him later.

"The Shifter Council?" She'd studied other paranormals hard. She'd had to in her lessons. But this one had escaped her. She was actually pretty clueless on how any of the paranormals on Earth ran their people. The thought of prodding Drey for more information filled her with excitement. She loved learning. She loved talking with others and finding out how things worked. Making this a perfect opportunity for her. Or maybe that was just the good feeling about the evening over all. It was definitely preferable to being stuck in the damn awful dress.

"Most paranormal communities have a Council. This is the shifter one."

"And they rule all the shifters?"

"Not really. Most of them, yes, but you tend to find that the various prides and packs sometimes have their own rules."

"Like the wolves that live with the fae?" she asked, thinking of the pack that'd lived with her people since childhood. As far as she knew, there were similar packs with the other fae, though rumour had it that the autumn wolves were out hunting their missing princess..

"A little. The lions seem to be the same, their prides have sub-rules, as do the dragon flocks."

"Dragons have flocks?" She cocked her head to the

side, considering the information. She'd never considered what a group of dragons were called. In fact, she'd thought they were mostly solitary creatures.

"Some do. Others are much more...grumpy around other dragons. There's actually one of the lone ones on the Shifter Council. He hates just about anyone and everyone though, so maybe stay away from him if you can." He laughed as he finished speaking.

"I hate to point this out, but I've no idea how to tell if someone's a dragon." Or any other kind of shifter for that matter. But she wasn't going to admit that yet.

"If he's glaring at me, it's likely to be Drayce. We're...uh, from rival flocks, even if he chose to leave his."

"That makes it sound very Romeo and Juliet."

"It is a little. You'd have thought it'd die off after a couple of centuries, but no such luck."

Centuries? Just how old was he? Was it creepy for her to be out with a much older man? Or was it okay because he was a dragon? She had no idea how any of this worked.

"Don't look at me that way. I'm not *that* old." He smiled reassuringly at her.

"How old?" The question came out like a whisper, and she dreaded his answer a little bit. Though him being older probably wasn't a big deal. Most paranormals were long lived, herself included, so it shouldn't be looked down on or anything.

"I'm thirty-three," he replied, and she breathed a sigh of relief. "But really, does it matter once you reach eighteen?"

"Not really, no," she replied, impressed that his thoughts echoed her own. They were right though. Paranormals aged a lot slower, and lived a lot longer, than humans did. So an age gap like theirs meant next to nothing. "I don't actually think about age much. Other than that this is the year I start doing the Birth."

"I've heard of that, it's a big ceremony, right?" It was his turn to look particularly curious. Aledwen liked that. It put them more on a level playing field in her mind.

"Yes. It's the transition of control between the Winter Court and us. I'm not sure how much it actually makes a difference. I think it's just the magic that needs guiding, but I don't know for definite."

"Why has no one ever told you?" he asked, before glancing out of the window, possibly to check where they were.

"I'm in the dark about a lot of things."

The car shuddered and she gripped onto the handle next to her seat, hoping nothing was going to go wrong with it. Drey chuckled again, and she threw him a glare. He shouldn't laugh at her. It wasn't *her* fault she knew nothing about the human world.

"There's no need to worry, Dwen. It's supposed to do that."

"And how am I supposed to know that?" she flung back at him. "I've never been here before, I've no idea how anything works."

She could have almost sworn that a tingle of magic passed over her skin as the anger rose. But she was probably imagining it. She couldn't do magic, and she'd been angry enough times before to know that wasn't what brought it on.

"I'm sorry, I didn't..."

"Yes, well."

The vehicle rolled to a stop, and without waiting for him, she flung open the door and got out of the it. Glad to have her feet back on solid ground. And glad she'd kept on her flat shoes. They were covered by her dress anyway, so she didn't need to worry about how they looked.

She glanced around, and a smile crept over her face. She could already tell how different this was to any of the parties back home. There was laughter about, and shouting. As well as a lot of different colours. And not one sight of a ball pink dress. Or a corset for that matter.

The women's dresses were sleek and elegant, fitting to their bodies closely and looking both comfortable and beautiful. Unlike the one she'd been wearing just hours ago.

"You okay?" Drey asked, coming to stand beside her and straightening the sleeves of his suit. There was something about a man looking as smart as he did that she appreciated. It spoke of effort, and pride, and a certain level of awareness of how he was presented.

Maybe it was the dragon in him. They could be particularly prideful creatures from what she'd heard. Then again, she wasn't going to complain about entering the ball on the arm of one of the most handsome looking men in there. Though she didn't know that for sure. There were probably other attractive men here. Maybe even an incubus or two. Everything she'd read about them, they oozed appeal, even if they weren't classically attractive.

"Just taking everything in," she replied, before turning to smile at him. For all his teasing, she really was grateful he'd brought her here. It was an adventure like she'd never had before.

"I forgot what it was like the first time." He smiled softly, and she almost forgave him for the earlier laughter. "You ready?" he asked, holding out the crook of his arm. She slipped her hand into it, smoothing her hand down the soft fabric of his suit coat.

"As ever."

Slowly, they made their way up the red velvet carpet leading up to a pair of grand double doors. Aledwen smiled to herself, anticipation building within her and causing a bounce in her step and a a soft hum to escape from her lips. She could feel satisfaction emanating from Drey, and it only sent her higher.

Coming here was a good decision. She had a feeling deep within her that it'd be one of the best decisions she made in her life. And that this was a turning point. Maybe she was imagining it. Or it was just wishful thinking. But ignoring a gut feeling never ended well according to just about anyone that'd done it. And Aledwen wasn't an idiot.

"Your names, sir?" the man besides the door asked. He was smartly dressed, in burgundy and burnished gold, looking every part the old world tradition. She tried to ignore the disappointment it caused. She didn't just want this to be another party like the fae.

Drey handed the man a card with something scrawled on it. She hoped it wasn't her actual title, that could cause a stir if it got back to the wrong people. Then again, the dragon shifter seemed smarter than that. He wouldn't do anything to out her so completely.

The doors swung open, and Aledwen's disappointment vanished. This was nothing like the fae balls. No one was really dancing for a start, rather, they were standing around talking and building alliances, filling the room with an enticing buzz. She wanted this. She could actually meet people.

An auburn haired woman over to the left, seemed to have attracted a large group of people around her, but was mostly ignoring them while choosing to talk to the darker skinned woman next to her. Their body language suggested they were friends, though maybe that was just the norm here.

"Dreyfus of Flock Kinnon, and companion Aledwen."

She breathed a sigh of relief at the introduction. No hint of her royal status meant she could just be a normal person here. There were no expectations, or extra eyes or anything.

"Is that okay? I didn't think you'd want to have everyone know?"

"Yes, thank you. It was very thoughtful," she replied with a smile. "I don't want anyone treating me any differently."

"I'm glad. What do you want to do first? There'll be dancing later. Or there's food. We can go talk to people. It's your choice."

He was so relaxed that it set her at ease too, and she leaned into him slightly. He unhooked his arm, and placed a hand against her back, sending her the reassurance she didn't know she needed.

"I'm not really sure. What do you normally do at these events?" She glanced up at him, only to be greeted by a slightly uneasy expression. But she said nothing. If he wanted to tell her, then he would in time. It wasn't on her to rush him. At least, not yet. Maybe later in their relationship it would be.

"Not come," he responded.

"Oh."

"They're fun and all, but dealing with Drayce...let's just say I'd rather not."

"Dare I ask?" She tried not to laugh, but a small giggle still escaped.

"He doesn't really like me much. Believes my grandfather stole a woman from him in the sixteen hundreds."

He shrugged nonchalantly and Aledwen tried not to freak out over how flippantly he spoke about so long ago.

"I don't see why that should make him hate you." It didn't make any sense to her. Not in the slightest.

"Me neither. But a lot of dragons, especially the older ones, keep vendettas for a very long time. It's how the wars just kept going."

"Like the fae war?" She thought back over what her tutors had taught her about the war between the Summer and Winter fae a few centuries ago. Well, really it was a war only played out by the Summer fae themselves. The Winter fae had tried to stay out of it.

"No, not quite like that. Actual fighting rather than battling it out with the weather," he responded.

"That's not what-"

"I'm sure it's not all that happened. Your people are private at best, and damn secretive at worst. Don't try and deny it, Dwen. You know I'm right." He was riled up, and probably not completely aware of what he was saying, not that it hurt any less to hear.

Even so, she knew he was right. The fae were exactly like that, even among themselves. She was a prime example of that.

"So, dragon war?" she asked, effectively admitting her thoughts to him.

"It's messy, and hurt a lot of people." His voice cracked, and realisation washed over her. She turned so she was facing into him, and placed a hand on his chest firmly.

"You lost someone?" she asked softly.

He nodded and looked away. "My mother."

"I'm sorry," she whispered. Seeing him like this made her chest tighten and she longed to make the situation better for him. Even if she knew she really couldn't.

"There's no need for you-"

"Kinnon," a voice boomed.

Aledwen noticed Drey's eyes narrow as a dark haired man strode towards them.

"Drayce," Drey replied, oddly stern.

"Can I have a word?"

Confusion crossed her dragon's face. "Sure, but I can't leave-"

"You have to." Drayce seemed pretty sure of himself, and Aledwen found herself nodding in acceptance.

"I'm fine. Go," she insisted with a smile.

Drey still looked unsure, but she gave him a knowing look until he nodded.

"Why don't you get something to eat?" he suggested.

"Yes, I am rather hungry." She wasn't actually sure if she could eat or not, but didn't want him worrying about her anymore than he no doubt would already.

"It's all over there." He pointed towards a long table at the back of the room. "I'll be back soon."

He looked at her with indecision written all over his face. It was almost like he was doing everything he could not to kiss her, and she couldn't decide if she wanted that or not. Regardless, the anticipation was there. As was the disappointment as she watched him walk away with the other man already talking quickly in his ear.

SIX

There was so much food, she wasn't sure where to actually start. If she listened closely, she'd probably even be able to hear the table groaning under the weight of it all. Rather decadent, and rather extreme. Probably too much so. Even the most elaborate party back home didn't have this much food available.

"You're supposed to eat it, not just look at it," an amused voice came from behind her, and she spun around quickly to discover who it was.

The man was tall and lean, but looked like he was still physically fit. A swimmer's body she believed it was called. It reminded her a little bit of some of the elves. Not unlike the representative of House Paige, but a little bit younger looking. His hair had a slight auburn tinge to it, though she guessed that could have been the lighting. Most striking of all though, was that there was two of him.

She shook her head. No, not two of him. Just twins.

Something had clouded her mind to the point she'd forgotten what the phenomenon was called. How annoying. She hoped that wouldn't happen again.

"I was just deciding what to eat," she replied truthfully. "Do you have any suggestions?"

Maybe she shouldn't be talking to two strange men at a ball, but she felt comfortable despite the company, and she felt it best to just go with it, especially while her backup was off talking to another dragon.

She giggled slightly. Her backup was someone she'd only just met, and yet here she was trusting him to protect her. How stupid could she get? In fact, this whole trip was a stupid idea, there was so much wrong with it. And so much right too.

"That depends what you like," he replied, a cheeky grin tugging at his lips. "I'm Brandon," he said, holding out his hand. She took it in her own, and gave it a firm shake.

"Aledwen," she replied.

"That's quite a mouthful."

"Using Dwen seems to be on the rise." She let go of his hand and gave a shrug. If one person was going to shorten her name, then others might as well too. And she didn't *really* mind Dwen. It was a lot easier to say.

"Okay then, Dwen. This is my brother, Cyprus, but everyone calls him Cy."

The other brother held out his hand and she took that too. His grasp was firmer than his brother's, and his face more serious, but she still found herself enjoying the warmth of his hand as they exchanged greetings.

"Good evening, Cy."

He nodded to her once.

"He doesn't really talk much," Brandon supplied, shrugging like it wasn't important. "And if he does, then you're truly special. He barely even talks to Mum and Dad anymore. Only Ari when they're alone."

"Ari?" she squeaked, a surprising amount of jealousy unfurling within her. Where was that coming from? She wasn't a jealous person by nature, and it seemed unlikely that two random twins should bring it out in her.

"One of our older sisters. She might come scold us if she sees us talking to you."

Cyprus smiled at his twin's words, and she just knew he was agreeing with the man. Though she wasn't sure how. It was kind of odd to think she knew what one of them was thinking and feeling. It made no sense.

"Why would she do that?"

"They have a habit of hassling pretty women," the auburn haired woman she'd spotted earlier interrupted. She smiled indulgently at the two men, and now they were all close, she could see the family resemblance.

"We weren't hassling, Ari, we were just talking to Dwen."

"Is that even your name?" Ari asked her.

"Yes."

"You're not a shifter?"

"No," she answered instantly, slightly offended by the question.

"Not yet, anyway," Ari replied cryptically. "As you were, little brothers. No causing a scene at my party."

With that, she strode away, leaving Aledwen completely flummoxed over what had just happened. She was pretty sure none of it made any sense to anyone but the other woman.

"Wonder what she meant by that," Brandon said, amusement colouring his tone. She guessed he wasn't worried about it in the slightest then. Somehow that wasn't reassuring.

"I was hoping you could tell me." True. She did hope they could shed some light on the words. There a theory playing on her mind, but she didn't want to think about that too much. While she did want love, and she wanted the truest kind, there was a big part of her that wasn't sure she was actually ready for it. Especially not if it meant a shake up of life as she knew.

Then again, that was coming the moment everyone figured out she didn't have enough magic to get through the Birth.

"So, any recommendations?" she prompted, turning back to the food laden table.

"Let us have a proper look."

Both of the brothers wandered up and down the table, pointing out things to each other, before exchanging nods and shakes of the head. She watched in fascination. Cyprus really didn't seem to speak, even to Brandon, and yet they were communicating with each other so seamlessly.

And she loved watching them. It was fascinating, and kind of beautiful. It was a bond that far transcended any other she'd witnessed.

Maybe that was just down to the rivalries that seemed to spring up between fae sisters. And the fact that fae brothers were looked down on for only being halflings. It was a stupid system. She'd have given anything for a sibling of her own. Someone to share the experience of growing up with, and getting into trouble with. A twin would have been perfect, but they just didn't seem to be very common when it came to her people.

"Here, we think you'll like this," Brandon said, handing her a plate that appeared to have some bread, apple and cheese on it. She frowned at him. That wasn't what she'd expected him to get. It wasn't opulent or fancy.

"Okay..."

"Just trust me, Dwen."

And weirdly, she did. She shrugged, and slowly raised the loaded up bread to her lips. She bit down, conscious of both the men's eyes on her as she did so. Hopefully the thoughts accompanying their gazes weren't too inappropriate. Though maybe she wouldn't be complaining about that at a later date. Something told her this wasn't the last time she was going to spend time with the twins.

She moaned slightly, the taste nothing like what she expected.

"See," Brandon exclaimed proudly.

She opened the eyes she hadn't realised she'd closed, to find them both staring at her with satisfaction written on their smug faces.

"What's so special about it though?" she asked between bites. No way was she leaving this behind.

"It's a local cheese, hand smoked. And the bread was made in the kitchen here."

"You must have a wizard in there," she joked.

"No, a rat shifter."

Unexpected, but she could live with it.

"So your sister said it was her ball..." she trailed off, hoping Brandon would get the hint and fill her in as to *why* the redhead had thought that. Cyprus just smiled knowingly.

"Not hers per say. She means the Council's."

"The Shifter Council?" Now that had her interest. If Brandon and Cyprus' sister was on the Council, it would mean she was a shifter. Meaning the twins were too. She found herself suddenly very curious about who was who.

"Yes. Don't you know where you are?" Brandon asked. He handed her another plate, this one had a few chocolates on. She put one into her mouth and almost moaned again. What was it with the food here? It was so much better than just about anything they had at fae parties. Or the rest of the time for that matter.

"Sort of..."

"They throw one of these every year," Brandon supplied once he realised she wasn't going to say anymore. "There's no real point to them, just a chance for a lot of shifters to come together. This is actually the first time Ari's let us come. Personally, I think it's because she's convinced her mate will keep an eye on us. But he seems a little preoccupied."

Brandon pointed over to the side where two large men appeared to be having an arm wrestle, the empty glasses by their sides revealing there was more than a little alcohol involved.

"That's his cousin-in-law. He was meant to be the panther alpha, but when his parents died, he ran away to the woods. He lives there now with Bjorn's cousin."

"And that's allowed?" Aledwen asked, her eyes widening. The thought of not accepting her responsibilities had never really been an option for her.

"Of course. Everyone has free will. Though it helped that his brother was willing to take on the role." Brandon turned back to her and smiled. "You're really not a shifter, are you?"

"Well, no. I'm-"

"With me," Drey half-growled.

"THAT'S OKAY," Brandon replied. "We were only talking."

"Don't get cocky just because you're a Reed." Drey's hands balled into fists, and Aledwen soon gave into the urge to place one of hers over it and try and offer him comfort.

To her surprise, Brandon laughed heartily.

"The name Reed would hardly protect me. My sister would throw me under the bus the moment I did something wrong. She may love her family, but she's not worked her entire life to get justice only to throw it away for us."

Aledwen looked at him in wonder, unsure whether that was something to be proud of, or something that just kind of made her a little bit sad. From the expression on Brandon's face, she decided that pride was the way to go. He was clearly impressed by his sister's passion and drive. She could get on board with that. Those were the same qualities she wanted to be known for when she became Queen.

Something told her she was going to get on very well with the twins' older sister. Which was definitely an odd thought. She'd probably never see the woman again after their brief interaction earlier. She couldn't sneak to the human realm regularly and stay undetected, as much as she'd love to be able to.

Drey said nothing, but he still glared at the other man.

"Stop it," she hissed at him.

"I can't," he replied through gritted teeth. Weirdly enough, she actually believed him. But that just made the whole situation all the more bizarre.

"What do you mean you can't?" she asked, feeling her eyes widen.

"Here's not the right place, Dwen," he replied, warily eyeing the twins. Aledwen sighed. She didn't like him seeming so dismissive of them. It hardly seemed fair.

"Okay, we'll talk about it later," she responded, already turning back to Brandon and trying to recall where they'd been in their conversation.

"We'll talk about it now, just not here." Drey's voice

was far more commanding than it had been before, and she wasn't okay with that.

"No," she responded instantly, and a look of horror crossed the dragon's face. At least he knew he was in the wrong, that did stand for something at least.

"I'm sorry," he said shakily after a moment's silence. "I'm not sure what's going on with me."

"That's okay," she answered, his clear distress softening something within her, but raising far more questions than it answered. She didn't want him to be bothered in the way he was, but she also didn't know how to go about making it go away.

Aledwen guessed she'd learn in time how best to cheer him up and make him stronger. Another odd thought to be having about him, admittedly, but she was going to go with it. Sometimes it was easier to go about life that way.

"It's not okay, Dwen. I..."

"It's fine, we'll talk about it in a little bit, let me just finish talking with-"

"Never mind us, Dwen," Brandon answered, her name rolling off his tongue like a caress. She liked it. A lot. But ignored it. One man causing weird thoughts was one thing, but two - three even - was just uncalled for. Other than a few experiments, just cause she was intrigued, she'd not really felt half the flicker of interest she had in these three. It was an odd sensation, but she didn't want to think about it quite so deeply. She'd do that later when she was alone in her bed mulling over the events of the evening.

"Are you sure?" She met his eyes, reassured by the swirling green irises that met hers. They were beautiful and captivating, but most of all comforting.

"Yes, we'll see you again." He winked at her, and a small giggle escaped, even as she tried to suppress it.

"I'm not so sure," she replied nervously.

"I am. See you soon, Dwen. Go sort out your smoking dragon."

Brandon turned away, and Cyprus gave her a quick wave before following. She lifted her hand to wave in return, more confused than she had been before.

She looked back at Drey and alarm coursed through her. Brandon hadn't been joking, he really had started to smoke. It was curling up from the corners of his lips and he was beginning to shake.

"Let's get you out of here," she said, tugging on his arm. Surprisingly, he followed. He just needed to shift. At least, that's what she kept repeating in her head. She just hoped she was right.

SEVEN

Even after the fast and furious flight back to the palace, Drey was still smoking, causing Aledwen to worry more by the second. She had no idea what the best way to deal with an angry dragon was. Or what an angry dragon would even do. If he shifted on her balcony then there was a good chance it would break and crumble, leaving her with a massive mess, and no way to clear it up.

"What's wrong?" she asked, wanting him to stop his anxious pacing already. She didn't say anything though. If that was what was keeping him human, then it was best just to leave him to it. At least, she assumed so. Her knowledge of angry shifters was somewhat limited to the past two hours or so.

"Nothing, everything, I don't know."

"Helpful," she muttered.

"I'm sorry," Drey offered, sighing.

"Are you though? Or are you just going to say that and keep steaming."

"You noticed that?" A worried look crossed his face.

"Hard not to, you're steaming up the windows."

"Sorry," he said instantly, glancing around at the glass she was referring to. She smiled to herself, amused by his reaction.

"Don't be sorry. Stop saying you are. It's obviously an involuntary reaction to whatever is getting you so riled up. Now sit down, and tell me about it. Maybe I can help?" She hated seeing anyone so worked up. And deep within her, she hated even more that it was Drey that was worked up.

"I don't know how to explain it."

"Then just try," she suggested, her curiosity right at the forefront. This was getting more and more intriguing by the moment.

"What do you know about shifter mating?"

Aledwen racked her brains. That hadn't been anything like what she expected, and it took her a little aback.

"Not a lot. Shifters mate for life. I guess that's about it, really." She shrugged, not quite seeing why it was important.

"I suppose that's the jist of it, but it's a bit more complicated," Drey said, finally sitting down on the sofa next to her. There probably about half a person's space between them, and Aledwen had to ignore the urge to move into that space so they were touching. It might even be a good idea if it offered him some level of comfort.

"It always is, fae mating is the same."

"Can fae mate with the wrong person?" he looked at her, an eager look that she didn't want to analyse, on his face.

"No. They can only mate with their fated one."

"Or ones?"

"Well, yes. But it's rare," she responded, though as she was saying it, she realised it might just be rare because most fae didn't get a chance to meet one mate, never mind more.

"And those mates aren't just fae, right?"

"Most of them aren't. There are no male fae after all. The male children are either half-fae or less.

"Ah. It's different for dragons. There hasn't been a dragon that didn't mate with another dragon for centuries, maybe even longer."

"Okay..."

There was something lurking in her mind that suggested there was something in what he was saying. But she wasn't too sure what. Or she was, but she didn't want to jump to conclusions and completely miss what he was trying to say. That was how things ended up awkward.

"I'm getting signals from you like you're my mate," he blurted out, and the lurking idea in her head nodded along. That was pretty much what she'd thought he was going to say.

"Alright..." She didn't want to say anymore, she

wanted to see where his head was at first. Pressuring someone into saying something they weren't ready for yet never ended well.

"But it makes no sense."

"Because I'm fae?" she asked, thinking back to his earlier question.

"No. Because I was getting the same mating vibe from your interactions with the Reed twins." He sighed, and rested his head in his hands.

"You think the Reed twins are your mates too?" That wasn't something she'd picked up on. In fact, she'd mostly picked up on amusement from Brandon's part, and jealousy from Drey's. Oh...jealousy...

"No..."

"You think they're mine too. And that's a problem?" She let the idea settle in her mind, surprised by how little it freaked her out. She probably should be considering he was telling her she'd gained not one, but three, mates in the past evening.

"Yes."

"But you didn't think you were mine until..."

"The moment I saw you standing with the Reed twins."

"Oh."

"It might be something to do with you meeting them. I know that's how mating one on one works, so maybe it's the same if there's more than one mate involved. But that's not the real issue."

"What is then?" she asked, taking a chance and placing her hand softly on his leg. If he *was* her mate, then maybe she could actually offer him some comfort. She liked that idea. And she really didn't like seeing him quite so worked up about things. It was disturbing to the core.

"You're not a dragon," he admitted softly.

"How much of a problem?" It made her nervous to think he might not explore something just because of what she was. And if that was the way all dragons were, then it wasn't really his fault. Even if it did suck.

"I don't know."

"Is it going to change how you want to act around me?" Her voice cracked a little, and she was surprised by the emotion that was lurking there.

"I don't think so." He didn't sound so sure.

"But..."

He turned to her, his dark eyes boring into her and looking pained. She lifted a hand and left it hovering above his cheek. She wanted to touch him. And she wanted to kiss him, to see if there really was anything between them, but something held her back. Or, not back as such, but it was making her particularly nervous.

Drey's eyes flitted down to her lips, and something clicked inside her. She wasn't going to know for sure until she actually did something about it.

She leaned forward, almost not believing she was actually doing this. It wasn't out of character as such, but she just wasn't normally interested like this. Instead of just being a kiss, whatever this was leading up to felt like more. It was important, she could feel it with all her being.

Slowly, she drew closer to Drey, and hovered with her lips just in front of his. All it would take was another small movement and they'd be touching.

Neither of them moved, their breath mingling between them and enhancing the importance of the moment for Aledwen. She wanted this. She needed some answers. Or more like confirmation really. If there really was something like a mating bond between them, then she'd have the answers anyway. She just needed the confirmation that she was right about that.

Taking a chance, she closed the small gap between them and pressed her lips against his. Within seconds, he was returning the kiss, soft and sensual rather than hot and demanding. Aledwen's eyes fluttered closed and she let herself get lost in the kiss.

One of Drey's hands snaked around her waist, pulling her closer to him. She smiled into their kiss. That wasn't the reaction of someone that wasn't interested. And from what he was saying, that meant they really were mates. Maybe there'd be some problems to come with that, but she was certain they'd be able to work through them.

She shuffled even closer to him on the sofa, not breaking the kiss as she did. She didn't want to lose contact with him unless she absolutely had to. The kiss they were sharing really was one to get lost in, and a large part of Aledwen was satisfied by that.

After what seemed like an age, but nowhere near long enough, Drey pulled away, and looked down at her with hooded eyes. There were a few moments of bliss before panic seemed to take over, and he pushed her away.

She slumped back into her seat, a rather unprincess-like position. She hated that he'd just rejected her so casually. Well, not reject, but definitely not accept the kiss they'd just shared.

"Drey?"

"I'm sorry, Dwen. I have to go." He pushed up from the sofa and strode towards the open balcony doors. Leaving her completely flabbergasted.

"Why?" she demanded, her voice coming out far stronger than she'd expected. Hurt would likely come later, but anger seemed to be her predominant emotion.

"I need to sort some things out."

"No. You need to sort this out, Drey. This isn't something to run away from."

"You think I'm running away from you?" He seemed hurt that she'd even suggest that, but given the current situation, she didn't think he had a leg to stand on.

"You're giving off that kind of impression."

"I'm not, Dwen. I just...have to sort some things out."

"But won't say what those things are, or why they suddenly appeared the moment we kissed." Her voice was almost raised. It would have been, if her royal training wasn't quite so thorough. That was all there really was standing between her and a shouting match. She wasn't even sure why it bothered her so much. She barely knew Drey still, there was no way she couldn't take this one personally.

"I can't tell you."

"Of course not."

"I'm sure there's fae secrets you can't tell anyone but your mate," he pointed out.

"Not really. I'm the princess, I'm not bound by those oaths." She'd always found that one odd too. Surely she was just as capable of spilling sensitive secrets as any of the other, more common, fae.

"I just can't yet. I need to sort something out."

"Fine." She turned away from him, and walked over to her bedroom, slamming the door behind her. While she tried not to, she couldn't help but hear the faint beat of wings as he left her balcony and flew back to his people.

When he returned, and she had no doubt he would, he'd have some major explaining to do.

EIGHT

S he was still mad at Drey. She'd tried not to be, he probably was telling the truth about having to sort things out. But maybe he should have thought about that *before* letting her kiss him. She felt like a fool. And no one made her feel like a fool.

Wow, that sounded conceited. Even to herself.

And it wasn't even quite what she meant. She just didn't like feeling the way she was right now. Like her kiss had chased a man away. And not just any man, but one who was quite possibly her mate. It was seeming more and more likely with each moment that passed.

Aledwen sighed, and turned back to the book on elvish politics she was trying to read. She was conscious that her meeting with the ambassador from House Paige was coming up, and she didn't want to seem completely clueless when he showed up.

While she was aware of the customs and Houses of his people, she wasn't aware of the actual politics. Apparently, the way other political systems work wasn't important enough to be a part of her education. She added it to the list of things she'd change when she was Queen.

It was probably time to start a list of things she wouldn't change. It'd probably be shorter.

"Princess?" A vaguely familiar voice drew her attention to the door.

"Yes?" she asked, looking up and not being surprised to discover the elf she was expecting standing in the doorway.

"I was wondering if you were ready for our meeting." While on the surface, he seemed calm and collected, some kind of vibe he was giving off had her convinced he was nervous. Maybe there was something in the treaty that the fae wouldn't like.

"Of course, why don't you take a seat?" She gestured towards the chair on the other side of her table, and closed the book she was reading firmly, sliding it to the side.

"Thank you."

He moved into the room and pulled out the chair so he could sit on it. He'd come with surprisingly little on him. Just a few sheets of parchment and a pen. It made her feel a little less under prepared. But only a little.

"That's very dry reading you've got," he said, nodding towards the book. It surprised her. She didn't think he'd comment on it at all. Or that he'd be the one to open the meeting. Which was possibly unfair of her. She didn't know him well enough to make judgments like that about him.

"I couldn't very well come to a meeting unprepared," she replied, surprised when he returned the smile she gave him. Despite herself, she found herself warming to him a little bit.

"I know how you feel. There's nothing like being taken totally by surprise."

"And yet, I suspect that's exactly what you're going to be doing within the next half hour," she joked.

"I'll try not to."

Weirdly, she actually believed him. "Aledwen," she said, holding out her hand.

"Not Princess?"

She shook her head. "I'd rather not, no."

"Fane, then." He took her hand in his, and something like magic felt like it was battering against her skin, causing a confused expression to flit across her face before she righted it again.

"Good to meet you properly, Fane."

"You mean without your mother?" he asked with a fakely innocent look on his face. Aledwen's jaw dropped. "Sorry, that was out of line," he added hastily when he noticed her expression.

"It's okay, I just didn't expect you to be so blunt about it. Doesn't make it untrue though." She hated thinking her mother had created such an impression. And that this was the legacy she'd be inheriting.

"She's a formidable woman."

"Yes," Aledwen admitted, not saying any more as she wanted to shut the conversation down. Without being rude, naturally.

"Did you find anything interesting in your book?" Fane asked, nodding back towards it. She was grateful for him changing the conversation. She'd begun to get uncomfortable.

"Not that I could understand. Your political system seems convoluted."

"That it is. It almost makes less sense than a monarchy based on the weather," he quipped.

"I suppose you may have a point there. But the systems are what they are. We can either try to understand that, or not. Personally, I want to understand it. I believe it'll make me a better ruler when the time comes. And able to forge better relationships with the other paranormals around."

"Well said," he acknowledged. "Want to practice now? If there's anything missing from your elvish knowledge, then I can fill you in."

"And you're okay with that?" she checked. She couldn't forget that ultimately he was here with a treaty, and therefore was automatically placed against her in the agenda they were working towards.

Kind of, anyway. She was sure his aims were similar to hers. That he wanted peace and something useful between their people.

"Yes, I'm okay with that. I feel like I might actually get our people somewhere with you at the helm."

"You should keep in mind that I don't have any power to make the final say," she pointed out, dreading to think what would happen if her mother overturned all of this. It was her prerogative as Queen, but that would mean nothing in Aledwen's heart.

"I know. But you can certainly argue our case."

"I can try." It was all she could really say, there were too many possible variables in play for her to say for definite one way or another.

"Thank you." He passed her one of the pieces of parchment, and she took it carefully, before pouring over it. Her brows furrowing together as she took in the words there.

"Is this for real?" she asked, shock coming through in her voice.

"Yes, unfortunately so."

"He realises what this means?" She couldn't believe what the elvish High Lord was after.

"Unfortunately, yes."

"It could start another fae war." She knew she was continuing to point out the obvious, but the shock was too much for her to actually handle.

"I feared as much. Is there any way we can avoid it?"

"Not if he wants to marry a fae princess. The summer and winter princesses are married already, and the autumn princess is missing. Which leaves..." It left her. She'd be the fae princess he was after. But that'd cause an imbalance in the fae courts, especially as she'd already reached eighteen.

"No."

"I'm sorry?"

"I don't want him to have you." Fane looked at her

with a mixture of admiration and confusion. There was clearly something odd going on.

"That's very sweet and all, but I guess it isn't your decision to make."

She re-read the treaty, dread twisting about in her stomach.

"Maybe not, but it is yours."

"Yes, it is," she acknowledged. "And it's something I can't go through with. But we need to find a way around that without risking starting some kind of war. I don't think your High Lord would take kindly to a straight out no."

"You're right, I don't think he would." Something dark crossed over Fane's face, and it was so at odds with the rest of how his demeanor had been that she was surprised to say the least.

"How well do you know him?" she asked, suddenly very intrigued.

"Too well. You don't want to end up with him."

"I don't want to end up with anyone I don't love," she pointed out.

"You're not a normal princess, are you?"

"Is there such a thing as normal?" she asked instead of replying normally. She wasn't even all that sure what he meant by her not being normal. What were princesses supposed to do in this day and age.

He chuckled. "No, I suppose there isn't. But I suspect even if there was, you'd still break the mold and be different."

She beamed proudly, that was something at least.

And she liked the idea he'd gained that much insight into her already. It said a lot about him too.

"I try. But what can we put in there that stops anything untoward," she asked, tapping a quill against her lips, and wishing she had a normal pen. Once again, the antiquity of court was just impractical.

"How close are you to being mated?" he asked slowly, his gaze lingering on her lips, before slipping down a little further. He looked back up at her face within seconds though.

"Erm...I'm not sure," she lied. It was getting a little confusing for her, especially as she was enjoying the attention Fane was paying her almost as much as she had Drey and the twins the day before.

"If you're close, that could be a way out of it."

"True, but also a trap. What if he insists on having me, and then I discover my mate? Will he just let me go?"

"I doubt it."

"And what are the consequences then? I've heard it's particularly hard to deny a mating bond. So I'd either have to sneak around, or go mad with unfulfillment." Neither of which sounded particularly great to Aledwen. Far from it.

"We could put in that he needs to release you if that happens?" While his suggestion was a valid one, it was completely undone by the uneasy look on his face. He didn't believe what he was saying was possible. Which meant it was probably best they didn't go down that route.

"How long have we got until he wants the treaty signed?" Aledwen asked.

"He wants it as soon as possible. I think he was hoping your mother would sign it without looking. She has a habit of doing that."

"Hence why you're wary of her?"

"Yes. She's signed away a few things she probably shouldn't have over the years." He shifted uneasily in his seat.

"Like?" she prompted, worry filling her.

"I'm not sure I should tell you," he said.

"Well that statement alone means that you have to." She narrowed her eyes at him, hoping he'd give in and tell her.

"I'm not completely sure about this, but I think there was a treaty that signed away some magic at one point."

A lead weight dropped in Aledwen's stomach. Magic. Her mother had signed away magic. If the other Queens found out about that, then there would be a price to pay. And Aledwen was pretty sure it'd be a steep one. Maybe even her mother's life. "Are you sure?" she asked.

"No. I've not seen it, there's just rumours about it. Hard to tell if they're true. A lot of the previous ambassadors have been highly swayable at best, completely corrupt at worst."

"That sounds...concerning."

"Oh definitely. One of them even made a deal with a rogue necromancer at one point. It caused absolute havoc within the community."

"It sounds like it." She sat back in her seat, pondering

the consequences of a necromancer having free rein anywhere. She'd heard that after a recent shake up, there were fewer rogue ones than there had been, but they also had no structure at the moment, and no one to hold the bad ones accountable.

Worrying to say the least.

"Yes," Fane acknowledged.

"What would he do with the magic he gained?" she asked.

"I've no idea. There should be no reason he can use it. I'm pretty sure only the fae can use fae magic."

"That's my understanding yes. At least, I've never heard of a non-fae being able to use our magic." She thought for a moment. That wasn't quite true. There was one non-fae who could use it, but she was pretty sure there was more to that situation that most people realised.

"Maybe that's why he wants a princess?" Fane asked, clearly still uncomfortable about the situation.

"It seems likely."

"What about the other things in the treaty?" he prompted, correctly guessing that they had exhausted that line of questioning. They'd add in the mate clause and hope for the best. Or hope Drey returned from his mope with the rest of the dragons. Yes, that was probably the best option.

"I think most of them can stay. But I'm not sure how we're going to provide him with access to dragon scales," she lied. There was a chance she *did* have access to those, but she wasn't ready to have anyone know that.

"Maybe it's from a different treaty," Fane suggested,

looking even more uneasy than before. Something rattled around in Aledwen's brain. He seemed very surprised by the contents of the treaty. Almost like he'd never read it before.

"Did you know what was in there before now?" she asked carefully, and Fane sighed.

"No. It was spelled until a royal touched it."

"Well isn't that awkward."

"Very much so. I'm curious by nature, so not being able to find out…"

"Plus, I imagine it's difficult to negotiate a treaty without knowing what's in it," she pointed out, an amused note in her voice.

"Ah, yes. Maybe I should have led with that." He looked away, the colour rising in his cheeks and up to the very tips of his ears.

"Maybe, but I like that you didn't," she replied.

And it was true. She *did* like and appreciate his honesty. It was a big difference from many other people about.

"I'm glad, because that could have been rather awkward otherwise."

She laughed.

"Very much so."

They lapsed into silence, both studying their own notes, though she suspected he was for the same reason as her. She didn't want to actually end their meeting, she was enjoying it too much, but she didn't know quite how to extend it without looking desperate.

A loud crash, followed by some particularly girlish

screams came from one of the courtyards outside, and Aledwen jumped to her feet. Not only did it break the tension, but she genuinely was intrigued by the cause.

She had a theory, but didn't want to hope she was right too much. Otherwise she could end up severely disappointed if she got there and discovered it wasn't Drey causing such a racket.

"Shall we?" Fane asked, an impish grin on his face. She warmed to him even more. If he was going to get involved with drama like this, then she could definitely get used to spending time with him.

"Only if we're done here," she said, mostly out of politeness. She was itching to go outside, but she knew better than to piss someone off who had the ability to make her life difficult.

"I think so. There's a couple of things I want to look into, if that's okay?"

"Of course, I don't control you." She flashed him a wide smile, and caught an interested look crossing his face in return.

"Yet," he murmured softly, almost as if the word was to himself and not to her. It probably was, so she chose to ignore it. There likely wasn't a good way of answering that one anyway. Though she did quite like the sound of it. "I'll be back in a couple of days," he told her, speaking loud enough for her to properly hear this time. She definitely wasn't supposed to have heard his 'yet' then.

"Days?" she squeaked, before scolding herself inwardly. That wasn't the tone of voice a princess should be taking. Far from it. "What's going to take you days?" she corrected in a more measured tone.

"I need to return home to look a few of the things up. But I'll be back, Aledwen."

Up until the point where he'd said her name, his tone had been all business like. But the softening had been unmistakable, and sent a little thrill through her. He could say her name like that any number of times and she'd be more than content.

"I'll see you soon," she said a little breathlessly. Why was she turning into such a girl? First Drey, now Fane. She'd add the twins in too, but they'd felt a little different to this. Comfortable, and charming, definitely. But different to this.

"Indeed, Your Majesty." He took one of her hands in his, and lifted it to his lips, placing a soft kiss on the skin of the back of her hand. The point where they touched began to tingle, but she dismissed it. All it was likely to be was her reaction to being flirted with.

Nothing more.

Anything more would just be a smidgen too complicated for her liking.

NINE

Aledwen's heart pounded as she skidded into the courtyard. Maybe she shouldn't really have been running. It wasn't a very proper thing for a princess to do, but there were too many screams for her to ignore now, and she'd be damned if she wasn't going to do something about it. Her duty as a royal meant she needed to do something. Well, it didn't. Not really. Or her mother would be here already. But her own sense of duty insisted she helped her people.

It took about two seconds for the scene in front of her to register in her head. Luckily, it did appear to be Drey returning that had caused the commotion. Her heart pounded for a completely different reason when she realised that. Not so luckily, it appeared like some of the guards were trying to subdue him. Why they thought that was a good idea, she had no clue. They may be wolf shifters, but he was in dragon form, and ten times the size of them all put together.

And Drey seemed enraged. There was already smoke rising from his nostrils, and she could have sworn she spotted a tiny flame at the corner of his mouth. This could end very badly, very quickly, but she wasn't entirely sure how to rectify that.

She began to walk forward, trying to look as sure and as purposeful as possible so no one interrupted her. This wasn't the time. It was too dangerous for them to. One lash of Drey's tail, or slash of his claws, and even one of the armored guards wouldn't stand a chance.

"Your majesty, no!" one of the attendants called out. Aledwen ignored him. She didn't have time for his over protectiveness, even if she did feel a little bad for dismissing him as easily as everyone else did.

Instead of listening, she took a few more steps forward, closer to Drey's thrashing form. If he wasn't careful, he was going to hurt someone, and she didn't want him to actually be responsible for that. From the Drey she'd seen and talked to, she doubted he'd be able to forgive himself easily. Even if he should. Even if she did.

"Back away," she called out firmly, aiming it at the wolves who were still vainly scratching at Drey's scales. A few of them listened, but the rest of the pack carried on regardless. "ENOUGH," she shouted loud enough that several of the other fae flinched backwards.

Good. They were about to learn what their future leader was actually made of. No more hiding away. No more being hidden. This was Aledwen's time.

One of the wolves, likely the alpha from the size of

him, shifted back into his human form, and faced her completely naked with a sneer on his face.

"Who are you to tell us what to do?" he snarled.

He was one of the wolves who hadn't stopped his attack then. She made a mental note to deal with him at some point. Especially when she became Queen. He'd give her hell at every opportunity if this was anything to go by.

There was a murmur around some of the fae, likely the ones who *did* know who she was. Why had her mother kept her so away from the rest of the world? If she hadn't, then Aledwen wouldn't be in the situation she was now.

"I'm your future Queen," she said firmly, and noticed Drey's head swing around, his large dark eyes staring into her. Good. If he recognised her for who she was, then it was definitely a good thing. It meant he wasn't just angry.

"I don't take my orders from princesses."

"You will if you know what's good for you," Aledwen said, trying not to flinch as the alpha stepped forward, crowding into her space and baring his yellowing teeth at her. She had some serious questions about why her mother kept him around now, but felt it was best just to leave those be. She couldn't imagine *anyone* would be very happy if she brought those up.

The alpha opened his mouth to speak, but a loud crackling, and the sight of orange flames licking past him, very nearly singeing his skin, made him close it again. Aledwen didn't look away from him, as much as she wanted to.

"Call off your men," she repeated, quieter this time. The last thing she wanted was to create more of an enemy than she already had. It wouldn't bode well for the future if she did.

To her surprise, the alpha waved his hand, and his wolves fell away, retreating back to where ever they spent their time normally. She had a sinking feeling she'd have to watch her back around them now. And that their animosity could have pretty severe consequences for her. But that was a risk she was going to have to take. *If* Drey was who he thought he was to her, and vice versa, and he ended up killed by the wolves, then things would end very *very* badly for Aledwen. As far as she was aware, mates would die without one another.

Making sure the coast was clear, she approached Drey, holding out her hand, though she wasn't sure why. He was well aware of who she was, she knew as much from the way he'd just protected her.

He settled down a little, thrashing a lot less, and sitting patiently on the stone ground. He must be cold. Wait, that was an odd thought. Why would he be cold? He was a fire breathing dragon, as she'd experienced just moments before. Cold probably wasn't in his vocabulary.

Reaching him, she touched her hand to the smooth scales of his neck, loving the feel of them under her skin again. She wasn't sure she was ever going to get used to it. She wasn't sure she ever wanted to. That way she had an excuse to keep touching him as much as possible. And *that* definitely sounded fun.

He swung his head around and presented it to her,

and she lifted her hand from his neck so she could stroke the side of his face. He nudged his head further into her hands, and she laughed lightly. "This would be easier if you weren't in dragon form," she said. He lifted his head up and cocked it to the side slightly, asking her a question she didn't know the answer to.

"Can you shift back?" she asked, slightly concerned that he hadn't.

Drey shook his head violently from side to side.

"Oh. Is it because of all the people?" She could feel them watching the two of them and wished they wouldn't, especially if they were giving Drey stage fright.

He shook his head from side to side again. Aledwen frowned.

"Okay, then we'll just have to find somewhere to put you where you'll be comfortable," she said.

He shook his head. This was getting worrying now.

"Drey, you're going to have to tell me what's wrong," she scolded, worry gnawing away in her gut. She didn't think she'd ever heard of a shifter getting stuck in their animal body before. Or not unless they were enchanted, but there was normally some kind of tell tale sign when that was the case. Drey was exhibiting none of those. He was just stuck in his dragon form.

Slowly, he lifted his wing and turned to look at it. She followed his gaze and inhaled sharply. There was a long gash on his flank, just under where his wing was situated. It must have been something ridiculously sharp to have cut through his scales like that, and she worried that an infection could end up setting in.

"Someone go get Diana," she called, not looking away from Drey and his wound. She didn't know enough to treat it herself, but the elderly physician would. Diana had been around for as long as Aledwen could remember. She'd fixed all of her childhood ailments and then some.

She'd also let Aledwen watch her prepare her potions and tisanes when she was younger. There had even been a time or two when she'd been allowed to help. Those had been good days, and childhood Aledwen had grown to look forward to them immensely.

"Now!" she barked when no one moved. Couldn't they tell that something wasn't right with Drey? Did they want him to end up with an infection? Even if they didn't care about *his* wellbeing, they should care about their own. She didn't imagine that an ill dragon would make for a great courtyard centre piece. A lot of people could end up hurt.

A great deal of shuffling behind her signalled that people were finally starting to listen to her. Good. They should, especially when it was for their own wellbeing. In the long run anyway.

"Can you lift your wing more, please?" she asked Drey, relieved to find him nodding his head in return.

She turned away slightly as he did, motioning for one of the fae by the well to bring her a bucket of water. Who knew why they even had a well, they'd had running water and indoor plumbing for as long as Aledwen could remember.

One of the women plonked the bucket next to Aledwen. "Thank you," she said, effectively dismissing the fae.

She leaned down, and ripped along the hem of her skirt. The fabric came away surprisingly easily, and elicited several shocked gasps from the eagerly watching fae. Aledwen rolled her eyes. This was likely going to be the gossip of choice in the grand hall later. Yey for her.

"This may sting," she warned Drey, who nodded his head in return.

She dipped the fabric into the bucket of water, hoping that both were clean enough not to make matters worse. Though she was sure Diana would arrive soon, and her own actions would be pointless. Saying that, she couldn't very well stand idly by while he was in pain.

She stepped in, close to the wound, the sweet scent of star anise assailing her.

It took a moment for Aledwen to realise what that probably meant, and she tried to tamp down on the panic rising within her. For all she knew, dragons were immune to poison anyway. Though he'd probably have healed already.

He flinched the moment the cool damp cloth touched his skin, and she winced for him. This couldn't be pleasant. She wouldn't like it if someone did it to her. Admittedly, she didn't have a wing joint complicating things. *Yet*, anyway. If what she'd heard about mating with shifters was true, then she might have at some point.

"What are you doing, Princess?" Diana's voice scolded, interrupted by the slight wheezes which suggested she'd run most of the way here. Aledwen would have commented on it, and that the older woman should take better care of herself, if she hadn't been too worried about Drey.

"I thought I'd clean out the wound," she replied needlessly, nodding towards the rag still pressed against Drey.

"Without a proper antiseptic? Do we even know what's in there?" Diana set down her bag and began sorting through her herbs and medicinals.

Not knowing what else to do, Aledwen removed the cloth from Drey's side, and dropped it back into the bucket, only then realising both would have to be burned. Quickly, she described her observations to Diana, who nodded along and muttered to herself.

"I need him to take this," she said, passing Aledwen a ball of sticky paste. "I don't suspect he'll let anyone else close enough to allow them to feed it to him."

"What is it?" Aledwen asked, her curiosity piqued.

"Family secret," Diana replied. "But it will purge the poison."

"Even in a dragon?" She worried her left sleeve as she realised the obscurity of what she was asking the woman to do.

"I can't say I've ever tried. But he seems pretty robust. If this doesn't work, we'll just try something else.

Aledwen felt rather than heard the low growl that came from Drey, and it made her chuckle.

"Well? No time like the present, Princess."

Contrary to how she felt just about any other time someone called her that, Aledwen actually liked it when Dianna did. Probably because it didn't come across as an honorific. Instead, she was using it as an affectionate name. And that made all the difference.

Aledwen faced Drey, his large, black, eyes watching her intently. She held out the sticky ball to him, her hand flat, like she'd hold it for a horse. The realisation of which made her frown. He wasn't a horse. He was a shifter. As intelligent as she was, if not more so, and yet she was treating him like an animal.

"We need you to eat this," she said softly. "It should stop the poison."

At least, she hoped it would. Every time they had to try something new, it would get more dangerous for him. Closer to whatever was in his blood spreading further and causing some lasting damage.

She wasn't okay with that.

He nudged at her hand, then carefully took the sticky ball between his teeth and threw his head back to swallow it down. It was amazing to watch, if a little stomach churning.

The effects were almost instant, and Drey began to sway back and forth at an alarming pace.

"I hope you're ready," Diana said, watching with a worried expression on her face.

"For what?" Aledwen asked, trying her best to hide her own concern. It wouldn't do for people to see her as anything less than sure of herself.

"I can't treat a dragon, Princess. He should shift back any moment."

"Shift back?!" she half-shouted. "Couldn't that kill him?" She gnawed on her lower lip. While it hadn't been long, Aledwen didn't think she was ready to give him up just yet.

Quicker than she expected, his scales retracted, and he shrank in size until he was human again. It was a sight to behold, and she wasn't quite sure how to take it. Seeing the wolves shift was one thing, but a dragon...well, they were considerably larger than humans. And that was probably an understatement.

Human Drey, thankfully still clothed, swayed even more than he had in dragon form, and she rushed forward despite the firm hand Diana tried to place on Aledwen's arm. But no one was going to stop her from getting to him.

Just as he was about to fall, she held out her arms and pulled him into them. He was heavier than she expected, but then shifters did tend towards muscly, but she just about managed to keep him upright. Carefully, she lowered him to the floor so she could tear up more of her skirt to use as a pillow.

Looking up, she spotted a couple of attendants still watching.

"Prepare a trundle bed in my rooms, please. And get Diana anything she needs."

Twin looks of shock crossed over the two fae she'd addressed, but they curtsied anyway, and ran off to do her bidding.

Aledwen turned back to Drey, and stroked her finger down his cheek. "We'll get you fixed soon," she promised, sure that was going to be the truth.

TEN

Aledwen watched as Drey's eyes flickered open, relief surging through her. He really was okay then. That was always a good sign.

"Hi," she whispered breathlessly.

"Hi," he returned, groaning low as he tried to move himself. The sound went right through Aledwen, and left her tingling all over in a way she'd never really experienced before. "Where am I?"

"In my room," she replied, thinking about the outrage it had caused to get him there. No one had been particularly happy about bringing him here. More fool them, really. It was far too late to protect her virginity, and he clearly hadn't been in any fit state to hurt her anyway.

He chuckled deeply.

"Yes, it went about that well," she told him, stroking a hand down his cheek and enjoying the smooth, warm skin against hers.

Hesitating for a moment, not wanting the same rejection as she received before, Aledwen leaned down and pressed a kiss against his lips.

It took him even less time than before to kiss her back, even going as far as tugging on her lower lip gently with his teeth. She moaned into his mouth, moving from the chair next to the trundle bed, and positioning herself on the mattress next to him.

She pushed her body against his, feeling her breasts press against his naked chest, only the fabric of her clothes between them. It was too much. She wanted them gone so she could feel skin on skin.

Where was this coming from? She was never like this. He just awoke something within her that hadn't been there before. She didn't want to admit how much she liked it just yet.

His arms snaked around her, pulling her closer to him. Not that she was complaining. He was so warm. So enticing.

Aledwen slipped her hand over the hard muscles of his chest, comparing how soft his skin was compared to his scales. She loved the feel of both, but this probably held the advantage.

Until he took her flying again. That could give this intimacy a run for its money.

She pulled back, looking down at him, his glazed eyes not really giving away how he was feeling.

"You okay?" he asked, brushing back a strand of long brown hair behind her ear, and trailing his hand down her cheek after letting it go.

"Yes," she answered, nodding along needlessly. But

her mind had gone a little blank, and all she could think of was Drey lying in front of her.

She didn't wait for him to say anything else, and leaned down to kiss him, pressing herself even more into his body. She filled her kiss with more passion than she'd ever imagined possible, and his hold on her body soon tightened. One of Drey's hands strayed to the lacing on the back of Aledwen's dress. She felt him tugging at the strings, and anticipation built inside her. She knew where this was going, and for the first time in her life she was truly excited by the prospect.

He pulled back from her, his face screwing up in concentration, still struggling with her laces.

"Do you need a hand there?" she asked softly, her voice coming out far huskier than she imagined it would.

"No," he replied instantly, resolve plain in his expression. But he was still struggling with the ties.

Even so, she left him to it. If there's one thing she'd learned over the years of only being able to watch life at court, it was that sometimes, letting a man believe he was needed and in charge, led to an easier time of it. They liked to feel necessary.

Aledwen applied that logic now.

"How fond are you of this dress?" he asked after a few moments more struggling.

"Not particularly." It was an awful colour, but comfortable and formal, perfect for the meeting with Fane she'd dressed for.

"Good." A wicked smile replaced the look of concentration, and a harsh ripping sound alerted her to what he'd planned.

A small giggle escaped from her lips as the dress fell away in two halves. The tattered fabric was a problem for later. As was telling him he wasn't allowed to rip her dresses every time he undressed her. So far he was two for two after all.

"Better?" she asked coyly, kissing him chastely before rising to her feet and getting rid of the rest of her clothing. She should feel self-conscious, and somewhere underneath it all, she did. But the feelings growing inside her far overshadowed that. Her only thoughts were those of Drey and the pleasure he could bring to her.

The pleasure she could take.

He really did bring out a different side of her, and she couldn't even bring herself to care. Maybe this was who she was really meant to be, and the slightly meeker version of herself was the shell before the man.

No. She stopped in her tracks. She wasn't ever going to be defined by a man. Any man. She was owning this moment because *she* wanted to. And if this moment ended, it would be on her terms.

The idea settled well within her, and she smiled to herself, pleased her realisation had come now, and not after she'd slept with him. The difference was only going to be a matter of minutes, but that wasn't the point.

Aledwen's skin heated as he gazed at her with hunger in his eyes. "Come back closer," he whispered, his voice hoarse with tension.

"Are you sure?" She smiled at him, surprisingly coyly for how out of the ordinary she was feeling.

"Yes, I want to taste you."

Jolts of desire shot through Aledwen as she removed the last of the space between them. "So you can eat me?" She almost covered her mouth with her hand, shocked at how forward she was being.

Drey chuckled throatily, his eyes never leaving her. "Only if you beg me to."

"Is that a challenge?" Aledwen cocked her head to the side, and attempted to look serious. Failing within moments. There was no way she could, not in this situation, when her body was desperate for his attention and crying out to be touched.

"Would you like it to be?"

She bit her lip, studying him intently. Did she? "What kind of game?" The words slipped out before she'd really considered if they were a good idea. But she trusted him, and knew he wouldn't do anything to actually hurt her.

"Let's see who begs first."

A soft whimper tried to escape from her, but she just about managed to stop it from sounding. Looked like she wasn't going to stand a chance. At least it was going to be fun to lose to him.

"And the winner?" Her voice cracked as she asked, and the anticipation was mounting by the second.

Drey sat up, surprising her with how well he'd already healed. He slipped his arms around her back, and pulled her into him, her bare skin touching his chest.

"Gets to choose where I take you first." He lifted a hand and tucked a stray strand of hair behind her ear.

Not wanting him to have any kind of advantage, Aledwen lowered herself onto his lap and cupped his cheek in one hand, guiding his face to hers and kissing him deeply.

She could feel him against her, making her smile against his lips. And get an idea. She dragged her hand over his clothed leg, and slowly drew it inwards. Drey's breathing hitched, pleasing her more than she really wanted to admit. There was something about knowing this was his response to her which had her feeling hotter than she ever had before.

And more beautiful.

She flattened her hand against him, rubbing slightly, and receiving more groans in return. A good response, but not begging.

She broke away from his kiss and pushed him back down onto the trundle bed, eager to get on with her devious plan.

Giving him a wicked smile, she kissed along his jaw, moving to his neck, and trailing kisses across his chest. She raked her nails over one of his nipples, receiving noises in response that travelled right through her. A good response, there wasn't any doubt about that, but it wasn't exactly begging.

Aledwen travelled lower, looking up at him periodically and meeting his hooded gaze. He was definitely as into this as she was.

With deliberate ease, she unbuckled his belt and

whipped off the rest of his clothes, leaving him gloriously naked before her. *This* she could get used to. She hoped he'd always be this willing in her bed.

Well, this was technically his bed, but she didn't want to get into specifics right now.

She kissed lower, swirling around his taut stomach with her tongue and watching him shiver with intense satisfaction. Luckily, this was turning her on as much as it was him.

Aledwen almost couldn't believe she was doing this, but she looked up at him, holding his gaze as she settled between his legs and took him into her mouth. It took mere seconds for Drey's hands to tangle in her hair, not pressuring her, but adding to the moment. And to the intensity she was feeling.

"Dwen...please..." he groaned, but despite the begging, she didn't stop. His reaction was too amazing for her to. She wanted to finish what she started now, no matter if he'd lost or not.

He shuddered beneath her as she swirled her tongue around him, a string of indistinguishable words falling from his lips.

"Dwen, stop."

The last word broke through everything, and it was as if a bucket of freezing cold water had been thrown over her head. She sat back on her heels, feeling exposed for the first time since they'd started.

"Did I do something wrong?" she asked in a small voice, already hating how far away he was.

She looked down briefly, and confusion filled her. He was clearly hard still, so why had he stopped her?

"What? No! Of course not," he assured her, and moved onto his knees before leaning in to kiss her, slipping his tongue into her mouth and teasing hers.

"But you said stop?" she looked at him in confusion after ending the kiss, not quite knowing how to process what was going on.

"Because I wasn't going to last much longer," he assured her, smoothing a hand against her cheek. "And because I need to show you how it feels. After that you can claim your prize."

"What prize?"

"You made me beg, Dwen. Have you forgotten already?"

Her mouth formed a little 'o', which caused Drey to run his thumb over it. Aledwen flicked her tongue out to taste it.

"No."

"Good. Lie back, Dwen," he commanded, but his tone was soft and fairly gentle. She was pretty sure that if she didn't want to obey, then he wouldn't make her. Which was comforting to say the least. And the main reason why she did as he asked.

The trundle bed was harder than her own mattress, but she didn't want to waste the time going to a better bed. Not when she'd be forgetting all about her discomfort in a matter of moments.

"If you don't like anything, you need to tell me." Drey spoke softly, and she nodded, wondering what he was going to do, and looking forward to finding out. "You're beautiful, Dwen."

She swallowed past a lump in her throat, her nervous excitement ramping up a notch. This was so much more than any of the other times she'd been with men. She wasn't entirely sure how she knew it was, but she felt it in her bones. This was special. This could very well be forever.

Soft kisses on the inside of her ankle chased all her thoughts away. The higher up her leg Drey got, the less coherent her thought got, even to herself. Her breathing became ragged, and she was vaguely aware of her chest already heaving. If this was the effect anticipation was having on her, what would happen when he actually got to the act itself.

She could hardly wait.

She didn't have to.

Drey pushed her legs wider apart, looking up at her as he did to make sure she was still comfortable. Or at least, that's what she hoped he was doing. Though he might have just been doing the same she did, and was enjoying the sight of her completely at his mercy.

He lowered his mouth to her, and she lost herself in the sensations that his tongue and lips were causing, a stream of unintelligible words and whimpers escaping from her. Including some begging, she was sure. But she also didn't care. Even if she hadn't won their game, she didn't think she would so long as he kept going and really didn't stop.

Deliberately slowly, probably to tease her more, Drey

slipped a finger into her, and she cried out, her body beginning to shake and shudder. He had to know she wouldn't last long now. She should be strong and tell him to stop, like he had with her. But she didn't. She couldn't.

The pleasure became too much, and she arched up into him, screaming out as it crashed through her.

It took a few moments for Aledwen to regain control of her thoughts, and she wasn't surprised to see Drey leaning over her, a satisfied grin on his face. He leaned down and kissed her chastely.

"Take me," she murmured.

"Are you sure?" he asked with a slight frown. But he didn't seem very convinced of his own words. She wasn't surprised. She couldn't say she was particularly convinced by them either.

"Yes. You said I could choose."

"Here?"

"Now," she replied. Really she was beyond caring on the exact location, so long as she could feel him moving inside her.

Seeing he wasn't going to do anything herself, she reached down and took him in her hand, causing a hissing moan to come from Drey. She smirked. That sound was worth it all.

She drew him to her, and then he took over, entering her with one firm thrust.

That was fine by Aledwen. Drey felt good. He felt right. Like they were both exactly where they were supposed to be.

ELEVEN

"You have to place your hands on the stone." Her mother scowled at her, and Aledwen just about managed to refrain from rolling her eyes.

Believe it or not, she *got* that she had to place her hands on the damned stone, because that's what she'd been doing for the past hour. "I am doing." She tried to sound as sweet as possible, aware that anything else would just rile her mother up more.

"You can't be doing it right. Step aside."

Hanging her head in shame, she backed away, her hands trailing from the stone and dropping to her sides. Dejected didn't quite cover how Aledwen was feeling right now.

Her mother placed both hands on it, and a soft green glow filled the room. "It's not broken then."

"I know it isn't," Aledwen replied. "But it wasn't working for me."

"Try again."

She sighed. There was no arguing with her mother when she was in a mood like this. She'd keep going until there was nothing else on either of their minds. It drove Aledwen mad. Even as a child. She needed gentle persuasion, not pushing to the point of exertion.

Even so, she placed her hands back on the stone, hoping for a miracle, but unsurprisingly not receiving one. How on Earth was she going to perform the Birth if she couldn't make the stupid stone glow. The ceremony required her to pull the power through herself and then do...something. She wasn't quite so sure what though. Over the years, when she'd seen her mother performing it, she'd glowed green and then it had just faded.

But her mother didn't really want to give up the power. The only reason she was passing the reins to Aledwen was because she had to. Tradition dictated that the Fae Princess of Spring took over following her eighteenth birthday. Now that had come and gone, there really wasn't anything that could be done. Not when it was a law written as far back as anyone could remember.

No one broke those rules.

Or no one that lived broke those rules.

She focused on the stone, willing it to glow, or do something. Anything. Even a short burst of light would be good at this point. Just some indication that there was life within it, then she could rest easy that the Birth was going to go to plan.

"I give up," her mother said, throwing up her hands

dramatically, causing Aledwen to scowl. This was completely in character. Things got a little tough, and her mother no longer wanted to deal with them. No wonder she'd been so absent during Aledwen's childhood.

Despite knowing her mother had left the room, and she was perfectly fine to stop, Aledwen didn't dare to. The Queen wasn't the only person worried about the ceremony. She wanted it to go well too, or else she'd end up being a laughing stock.

"Still not working?" Drey's low voice caused butter-flies in her stomach, and while she shouldn't, she turned around to look at him, smiling broadly. She had no words to describe how amazing yesterday had felt for her. What it had unlocked inside her. Probably because she didn't quite know what had changed. Just that she liked it.

"No." She dropped her hands to the side.

"Let me try something?" He sounded genuinely curi-ous, so she nodded. And not just because she wanted him closer to her, though that was a definite benefit.

Drey stepped up behind her, and slid his hands down her arms, leaving a trail of goosebumps in his wake. She pressed herself back into him, feeling his hot breath against her skin.

"I'm going to put my hands over yours," he whispered into her ear, and she nodded, willing to try anything she could to make this work.

Their fingers entwined, and Aledwen focused on matching her breathing to his, not knowing if it would actually help with what he was trying to do, or if it was just a way of comforting herself. The latter seemed far more likely.

"Try again."

"Sorry?" she asked, not quite knowing what he meant.

"What you were doing before, to try and make the stone glow like your mother did? Do it again." His words were firm, but gentle, filling her with a hope she hadn't had before.

Slowly, she tried to draw the power, feeling a slight prickling sensation in her fingertips. That couldn't be right, could it? Why was it doing that? From all her reading and research, using magic shouldn't hurt at all. Rather, it should make her feel more complete than before. Make things easier so to speak.

Unbelievably, the stone began to glow ever so slightly. Though not as brightly, or as evenly as when her mother had drawn the power. She wondered why that was. Maybe it was because Aledwen didn't seem to have any magical powers of her own. Or maybe it was something completely different.

Or it could be related to the deal Fane had mentioned. She shivered. That was a concerning thought.

"Are you okay?" Drey whispered, making Aledwen curse inwardly. She hadn't meant to make him aware of what was going on in her head.

She pushed his hands out of the way, and removed her hands from the stone, the patchy green light disappearing far quicker than it had arrived. Turning around in Drey's arms, she looked up at him with annoyingly adoring eyes. While she was sure of the emotions she was feeling, she didn't want to become one of those love struck women who became shells of their former selves just because there was a man around.

One day, she was going to be a Queen. And she wouldn't be one ruled by her mate. Nor would she rule her mate. Rule Drey. That wasn't how the relationship she'd imagined for herself had ever gone. It wasn't how any relationship should go. But what went on behind the closed doors of others was really none of her business.

Or at least, she kept telling herself that.

"Dwen?" he prompted after she'd been silent for slightly longer than she anticipated.

"You're the only person to ever call me that," she replied instead of answering his concern. There was no real easy way to explain all the thoughts and feelings swirling around her head. Maybe one day she would.

"Don't you like it?" He frowned down at her, and despite the seriousness of the moment, her gaze slipped towards his lips. Flashbacks of the night before sprang to mind.

"I do. It's just..."

"Just?"

"I've been so sheltered, for so long, that it feels like no one's ever really known me," she admitted.

"But I do." He sounded very sure of himself.

"Well, not yet. But you feel comfortable." She wouldn't lie to him. He felt right, and he felt comfortable, but they didn't know each other yet. She was sure that would come with time though. Which was always a good thing.

"I can live with that," he murmured, lowering his face to hers and pressing a soft kiss against her lips. Aledwen didn't waste any more time, and slipped her arms around his neck, pressing her body into his and deepening the kiss. The connection between them was definitely real.

To her surprise, he let her have control. Though that might not be a good thing if she started stripping him off right here in the throne room. While she was pretty sure her mother was done for the day, and wouldn't be returning, the room was still public domain, and as such anyone could walk in.

With that realisation, she pulled back, breaking the kiss, and leaving them both breathing heavily.

"I wonder if I'll ever get used to that," Drey whispered, brushing his fingers against his lips.

Aledwen mirrored the gesture, finding her lips slightly tender from the force at which she'd kissed him.

"Do you mind if I try on my own?" she asked, gesturing behind her at the stone. He nodded once, looking ever so slightly taken aback that she'd stopped their kiss and turned things back towards business.

"Be my guest." He stepped back to give her a little more space, and with mounting dread, she placed her hands back on the stone and tried to draw her magic again.

This time, there a tiny glimmer of green. No more than a spec in the grand scheme of things. But it was more than she'd had previously, and that was all that mattered. For now, anyway.

"Did you see?" she asked, excitement weaved into her tone as she looked back around at Drey.

"I did." A look of concentration flashed over his face, and she wondered what that was about. "But it's supposed to light up completely, right?"

"Yes," she admitted, dejection welling up inside her again. A couple of glimmers just weren't going to cut it. "I don't know what to do, Drey." She felt the tears prick in the corners of her eyes, but blinked them away. She wasn't going to cry in front of him. Especially not over a stone of all things.

"I think I have an idea. But it'll only work if you'll trust me."

"I do," she answered instantly, not even considering whether it was the truth or not. Deep down, she knew it was, and that was enough.

"There's another ball tonight, right?"

"You know there is. There's one every night until the Birth." She gave a weak smile, amused by his questioning of something he clearly knew already.

"Then I'll be back in time for a dance. But trust me, Dwen. I'll find you the solution you need."

"I hope so, I've been looking for years, and not found one."

He frowned at her. "Then I think my solution might actually be the right one." He leaned down and kissed her softly, lingering for just a moment. "I'll be back soon."

"I'll see you then." She waved at him as he turned

and left the throne room, leaving her alone with the stupid green stone. It'd never worked at all for her, so seeing a few specks of green was a good start, if not quite good enough for what she needed. And damned if she was going to let Drey be the only one finding a solution. Back to the library it was for her.

TWELVE

A nother wasted day in the library. If anyone could call time in the library a waste. Being so surrounded by books wasn't as far as Aledwen was concerned. But it also hadn't turned up any of the answers she'd been hoping for. At least it hadn't raised any new questions. Unlike whatever Drey was up to. That had raised a lot, and she was dying to know what he was up to.

Unfortunately, he was yet to return. Or if he had, then he hadn't made himself known to her. Which was disappointing to say the least.

And so, she found herself crammed into another awful gown. Though this one was slightly less terrible than the pink monstrosity of a few nights back. Maybe she could get Drey to rip through this one too. Eventually, there'd be no awful gowns left, and she'd be able to wear what she wanted.

Aledwen snorted. Like that was going to happen

before she became Queen herself. If there was one thing no one messed with, it was the current Fae Queen of Spring. Or the previous Summer Queen come to think of it. Though the woman hadn't been the same since she'd tried to steal the powers of winter and been defeated. The new Queen, Rose, was a much better fit for the prosperity of all four fae courts.

The ballroom was teaming with people, as was to be expected. Even the Spring Fae living in the human world came back for the celebrations leading up to the Birth. There was something about it that seemed to infect everyone with a kind of party spirit. Which would have been fine, if Aledwen had been able to enjoy it. This year was better as she could at least attend, but previous years had been a complete waste of her time.

"May I have this dance?"

"Fane?" she asked, spinning around so she was facing him. She hadn't meant to seem surprised, but after he'd left earlier, she didn't expect him to be back so soon. She also hadn't been expecting the butterflies that'd taken up residence in her stomach. What was all that about?

"Dance?" he asked again, holding out his hand.

Aledwen took it and he drew her into a hold, leading her through the simple waltz playing with a practiced ease.

"What did you find out?" she whispered after taking a few moments to truly enjoy the moment. She liked to dance, and she didn't often get the opportunity to do it.

"Not much. It's as I suspected. One of your mother's earlier deals signed away your magic."

Aledwen swallowed loudly. "But why?"

"She did it before you were born. My guess is either she didn't read what she was signing away, or she didn't think she was ever going to have a child."

"Seems like a stupid risk to take," Aledwen muttered, trying to ignore the stab of hurt lodging itself in her heart.

"Very much so. There's no explanation of it."

"But why would your High Lord even want a fae princess' powers? They should be useless to him."

"They are. But I think it's a long run game for him. There's a clause in the treaty that says marrying or mating with an elf will return the powers."

"So basically, he was using the treaty to force a marriage alliance. But what does he have to gain from that?" She really was struggling to work it out. There wasn't a history of either friendship or animosity between their peoples, so it made no sense for this to be coming up now.

"It sounds like it. And I really wish I knew. Maybe he was hoping for a weak princess he could mold to do his bidding? You're not exactly magically weak."

"I think you'll find I'm magically nothing," she pointed out.

"Yes, but if your mother hadn't signed the treaty, you would be."

"What can I do about it?" She hoped he had some kind of answer. And that it would help if she mixed it with the odd magic bursts in the throne room earlier. So far, no one had really cottoned on that she had none. Or maybe no one mentioned it because they thought it was weak, and she'd be funny about them commenting on it.

No matter the reason, it wasn't widely publicised that she had no powers.

"Short of finding an elf to mate or marry, I doubt there is anything."

An uneasy look crossed Fane's face, and he looked away quickly. Suspicious, but she'd let him have it for now. Especially as he'd been helpful in other ways already.

"What did my mother get from the treaty in return?" she asked instead of prodding more. Treaty seemed like too nice a word for something so restrictive, but Aledwen let that one slide. Here and now wasn't the right time to bring it up.

"Aledwen." Her mother's voice cut through the conversation. *Speak of the devil, and she will come.* Always seemed to be the way. Fane looked at her before shrugging and letting her go, slipping back into the crowds without anyone really noticing. Aledwen wished she could do the same. Anything to avoid whatever talk her mother was about to give her.

"Your majesty," she said formally, curtsying politely.

"You were talking to the elf." The look of disdain on her face made her feelings plain. Aledwen chose to ignore that.

"Yes, we had an interesting discussion about the treaty he's presenting," she responded, watching her mother's face closely to see how she reacted. Unfortunately, she stayed as passive as ever. Aledwen just had to hope the expression wasn't one she'd inherit.

"How so?"

"Part of it involved a marriage."

"Good, good. So I'm signing it tonight?"

"No!" The word slipped out before she could stop it, but even so, she couldn't regret using such a strong tone.

"Excuse me?" The Queen blinked a few times, trying to make sense of what she was hearing.

"You can't sign it."

"Why ever not?"

"It gives me away and forces me to marry," Aledwen said, just about as calmly as she could manage, but probably not managing.

"It does what?" She was surprised to hear Drey's voice, but not the cool, controlled anger in his voice. That was very much expected. And very much welcomed. Saying no to her mother alone was becoming nerve wracking, Drey would give her the extra confidence to carry it on.

Not that she turned around to look at him. She didn't really need to, she could sense his presence near her, further convincing her that there was something between them.

"There's a treaty that if signed, will force me to marry the elvish High Lord," she explained calmly, and could have sworn she heard crackling behind her. Maybe Drey was even sparking. That wouldn't be good. She was wearing a lot of flammable material, as were many of the other fae in the room.

In fact, calming him down should become her first priority. Ignoring her mother, she turned and almost took a step back when she realised Drey wasn't alone. Not that it was a bad surprise. Quite the opposite. The auburn haired twins stood to either side of him had her heart leaping and anticipation building.

And not just because they were looking so angry on her behalf.

Aledwen could feel the stares of the nearby fae on her as she closed the small gap between them. She touched her hand to Drey's chest, while holding her other out to Cyprus on the other side. He took it eagerly, and she instantly regretted not having three hands for all three of the men.

She looked up into Drey's dark eyes, finding them boring into her with a possessive intensity. He was going to have to deal with that possessive side at some point. She wasn't the kind of woman that would bow down to it. Not by a long shot, and it was better he understood that now, and not a lot later.

"It's not being signed."

"I need that treaty," her mother interrupted sharply. "I can't not sign."

"Dwen is *not* signing any treaty," Brandon growled, stepping between Aledwen's turned back and her mother, as if to protect her from something undefined.

"Who are you?" Her mother was getting shrill now, and something began to tick away at the back of Aledwen's mind. They were in public, and this wasn't the best way to be representing themselves to their people. Not by a long shot.

"It doesn't matter who he is," she answered in Brandon's stead. "But if we're going to have this conversation, can we withdraw to the consultation room."

"Good idea," Drey replied, his voice already sounding softer as he looked at her. She smiled at him, a secret one that was just for them. And maybe for Brandon and Cyprus too. She'd probably have to have a conversation about that with them at some point. Wouldn't that be fun.

Well actually, it might be. The twins had come with Drey to the ball after all.

"Fine."

She felt, rather than saw, her mother storm off, but was distracted by Cyprus tapping a single finger on her arm. She nodded at him, fairly certain he was asking for a moment alone.

"We'll catch up," she told Drey, knowing she didn't need to tell Brandon at all. He knew his brother, and she imagined he already knew about what was going to happen now.

Once they'd left, Cyprus did the only thing she hadn't expected him to, and pulled her into his arms to join the softly swaying couples all over the dance floor. The song playing wasn't one with proper steps, which was probably a good thing given how pent up she was.

"You're probably wondering why we're here," Cyprus said, taking her aback. Okay, there were two things she hadn't expected him to do.

"Just a little," she replied, trying her best not to blurt out a question about him talking.

"I can see the question in your eyes, Aledwen."

"You used my full name." Because *that* was a great response. So eloquent and informative.

"Someone has to. Everyone else seems to have forgotten it."

Aledwen laughed. She hadn't thought about it like that. "Now you mention it..."

"I can call you Dwen if you'd prefer..." He was quick to counteract with the statement.

"Only if you want to, I don't mind." And she was just honoured that he was talking to her at all. She'd had no problem believing what Brandon had said about him only ever talking to Arabella.

"I like Aledwen, it makes us different."

"You don't want to be like your brother?" That surprised her. They seemed so together in just about everything they'd done so far, that it surprised her to find out they wanted to be different. She chastised herself for that one. Of course they were different. Just because they were identical didn't mean they were the same person.

"Most of the time. But I don't want our relationship with you to just be as one item. We'd be three people in it."

"Four, if you count Drey," Aledwen added, before instantly wanting to recall the words. Why on Earth had she said that? She might be feeling the same sense of trust and connection to the twins as she did to Drey, but that didn't mean they felt one to her. She shouldn't just assume that would be the case.

Cyprus chuckled softly. "I see you get where this is going."

"You want me to be in a relationship with all of you?"

"If you didn't, you'd already be running away right now."

"I guess so."

"When you think about being with us all, how does it feel?" he asked gently.

"They've elected you to have this conversation with me, haven't they?"

Cyprus smiled at her, a smile that told her she was spot on in her assessment.

"They figured I was least threatening."

"And the fact you wanted to talk to me at all convinced Brandon?" she teased.

"Yes. Though our parents are going to take a lot more convincing when the time comes. They weren't pleased that Ari mated with a bear, so I'm not sure how they'll react to you being with both of us."

"I guess that's not really their choice though."

"That's not a no to all of us, Aledwen."

"You're right, it's not."

He broke the conversation by spinning her under his arm, and she twirled, loving the way her skirts moved, even if the dress itself was horrible.

"If you're comfortable with it, then the three of us have your back."

"Three..." she whispered. Something about that

number seemed off, and her eyes scanned the room, searching for something, or someone, but she wasn't sure what.

"Or more?" Cyprus prompted, making Aledwen laugh.

"Up until a few days ago, I had no love life to speak of at all, now I have more than one woman should dream of."

"Funny how the world works." Except that he didn't sound like he actually found it amusing. There was something very off about the expression on his face.

"Something about the reason you don't talk much?" Maybe she should have left the question unasked, but a part of her was dying to know the reason. Clearly it had affected him, and she longed to know why, but knew it would take time.

To her surprise, he nodded. "I'll tell you one day."

"When you're ready," she responded.

"I will. Your answer now has helped a lot with making sure it's not an issue again."

That was cryptic, and had her brain working at a hundred miles an hour. Maybe it was something to do with a woman? If he'd tried to share with Brandon before, and it'd gone badly, that could explain his hatred of talking.

"So long as you feel good about this too." She broke his hold ever so slightly, and lifted a hand to his cheek, rubbing her thumb against his soft skin. Yes, she was definitely okay with having them all. Things between her and Drey were great, but she could also feel a connection

to Cyprus, and no doubt to the brother who took the spot-
light a lot.

"I feel very okay with this," he murmured and leaned
down, pressing his lips against hers. Something awoke
inside her. Not the burning passion like it had with Drey,
but something softer, more loving.

Cyprus was gentle, and the admiration he already
seemed to have for her shining through in his kiss.

She didn't care they were in a ballroom full of people.
For the first time in her life, she felt like a proper princess.

THIRTEEN

A s little as she wanted to leave the moment she'd
shared with Cyprus, she knew she had to go sort
the mess with her mother out. Especially if she didn't
want to end up married. Why had her mother signed that
first treaty? She'd love to ask, but she didn't want to in
front of the guys, it seemed unfair to bring them into
something like that straight away. They were angry
enough about the marriage thing.

She walked into the room, Cyprus' hand in hers more
comforting that she wanted to let on. She was nervous
about the confrontation over this. It could end particularly badly for them all. Especially if her mother had
actually known what she was doing when she'd signed
the past treaties.

A low growl filled the room, and she looked around,
half expecting to discover a shifted dragon to be filling the
room. Except that the noise wasn't coming from Drey, it

was coming from a slightly larger than normal fox in the middle of the room, its teeth bared towards her mother.

"Call it off," the Queen shrieked.

"Brandon, please don't eat my mother," she asked, and watched in awe as he shifted back instantly, leaving him gloriously naked.

Aledwen's gaze slipped downwards, and she found herself inappropriately wondering if the twins were identical in this way too. If so, she was in for quite some nights ahead.

Realising the direction her thoughts had taken, a blush rose to her cheeks and she tore her gaze away.

"Here," Drey said, handing Brandon his jacket. "Probably best you don't talk to your mother-in-law naked."

That should freak her out. The mother-in-law part, not the naked shifter part, but for some reason it didn't. Okay, not some reason. She knew why she was feeling that way. Cyprus had covered it in their conversation before coming to the room after all.

"What happened to your clothes?" she asked.

Next to her, Cyprus' chest heaved as he laughed, clearly more than just amused at his brother's predicament.

"I...errr...had a little accident." Brandon scuffed his feet against the floor, looking down at them as if they were suddenly the most interesting thing in the room.

"He exploded out of them," Drey supplied, gesturing to the scraps of clothing littering the floor.

"How come you don't do that when you shift?" she asked curiously, forgetting her mother was in the room.

"I had my clothes enchanted by a genie."

Well, that hadn't been what she expected. She hadn't even known that genies were real. It made sense. Most of the creatures from the human tales actually existed, just not in the way the stories told them.

"Makes sense," she said offhandedly.

"What is going on here?" her mother demanded. Oh, oops. Aledwen had forgotten she was even in the room. Apparently being growled at by a fox was enough to keep her quiet. Aledwen would have to remember that for future arguments.

"I think you're meeting my mates," Aledwen said, surprised at how easily the word slipped off her tongues

"Your mates, Aledwen? Really? That doesn't seem likely."

"Why? Because you've never let me out of the palace? Or because you didn't think I'd be able to win anyone? Or maybe because you actually *want* to marry me off to an elf for whatever reason is behind your treaties." She didn't know where any of that came from, but she knew it needed saying. Kind of.

Her mother stood stock still, staring at her with a confused expression on her face. At least, it was confused before it became enraged. "What did you just say?" Her voice dripped with cold anger, causing dread to spread through Aledwen.

Cyprus squeezed her hand, and she relaxed a little. it was definitely helping having him there. It was helping having all three of them there. She wasn't alone now. She needed to remember that.

"I know about the treaties. I know they've been going on since before you were pregnant with me."

"And you're trusting that elf over your own mother?" she sounded genuinely taken aback by that.

"No, I'm trusting my own eyes. I saw the most recent treaty. I *know* what it says." Aledwen was almost shaking with anger now. Her mother had messed with her life and didn't even realise she'd done it. That wasn't fair to either of them really.

"Oh."

"What do you get out of signing these treaties blindly, mother?" Aledwen asked, completely on edge. Confrontation was awful, and she hated it any time it came up. Yet, she needed some answers, and where did her loyalties lay? For her mother, who'd raised her and was ultimately her Queen, or to herself, who she'd have to live with for the rest of her life.

"It doesn't matter."

"I think it does," Aledwen replied, along with a low growl from Brandon. She could almost swear she saw orangey-brown fur flash over his torso. Good to know he had a little bit of a temper, if she knew, then she could do her best to help keep it under control. Hopefully.

She waved her hand at him, in a gesture she hoped said she had this handled. Though she wasn't a hundred percent sure she did. But it was her mother, her problem.

"It's none of your business, Aledwen," her mother tried instead.

"While it's my magic, and my marriage on the line, I think it damned well is." She only just managed to keep from shouting the words. But she really didn't want any of the other ball goers to overhear and come watch. That would be a disaster.

Plus, they'd probably check Brandon out, and Aledwen was *not* okay with that.

Not at all. He was hers.

"Your magic, Aledwen?"

"You have absolutely no idea what you've signed away over the years, do you?" Cold rage travelled through her. How in all the realms had her mother not realised what she was doing? How had she been so careless with the future of her daughter and her people?

"I..."

"How many treaties have there been?" she demanded, wanting to know just how much damage her mother had done.

"Five."

"What do the others say?"

Cyprus squeezed her hand, offering his silent support. She wondered if he'd speak when there were other people around too, or if that was just for when the two of them were alone. She suspected the latter, making her feel honoured and more than a little loved.

Loved? Oh no. Way too early for that. She pushed the thought away. Definitely not time for that.

"I don't know."

"Get out," Aledwen fumed. If she'd been a dragon

shifter like Drey, she was sure she'd be smoking at the mouth right now. Concerning to say the least.

"Aledwen…"

"Out, now! And not just of this room, don't go back to the ball."

"You have no right to order me about," her mother protested, but the look on her face said it all. She knew she was beaten, and she knew Aledwen had support.

She probably also knew that the fae wouldn't stand for this when they discovered it.

"You have no right to sign away my future without even reading it." She turned away from her mother, no longer wanting to look at her face. "Drey, I need you to go find me Fane Paige. I have to speak with him now."

"Got it." He nodded once and walked out of the room. Hopefully he'd find the elf quickly, and they'd be able to start working it out.

"Drey," she called. He looked back over his shoulder, showing he was listening without saying a word. "Bring him to the library. I don't want this conversation where anyone can overhear."

He nodded, and continued walking.

"Aledwen…" her mother pleaded. Aledwen turned to her and glared in a way she didn't even think she could achieve. Turned out she could do it though, as her mother flinched backwards.

That was odd. How had she never realised how weak her mother was? She'd always come across as this stern and foreboding, but now…

"Leave. Now. Don't go back to the ball, and don't come near me until I say it's alright to."

"And just how are you going to ensure that?" she sneered slightly, but there was still a hint of fear in her eyes.

"I'll watch her," Brandon offered instantly.

"Are you sure? I..."

"I know. I should be in the library with you, but someone needs to watch her, and I know Cyprus will watch out for my interests."

Aledwen nodded. "Thank you, Brandon." She didn't like it. She'd much rather know her mother wasn't going to be able to get up to more mischief than have Brandon with her. Weirdly, she trusted him already, far more than she probably should, but she guessed that was the bond between them. There was no denying what it was anymore.

"Thank you." The urge to kiss him was strong, but she held back. Not because it was wrong to, but because she didn't want their first kiss to be in front of her mother. "Let's go get some answers," she said to Cyprus, making her way towards the door, and towards the library where Drey and Fane would hopefully be waiting.

Her stomach flipped at the thought of the two of them together, though she did her best to ignore it. She'd explore the idea tomorrow, when she had more time.

FOURTEEN

S he sighed in relief when she saw both men sat at the corner table, with the fire blazing next to them. Perfect. The only thing that would make it better, was if she actually had comfortable clothing to wear. But it was win some, lose some she guessed.

Cyprus' hand was still warm in hers, and she didn't want to quite admit how much she loved it. At least not aloud. Though he probably already knew.

"Ah, you're here," Drey said, rising from his seat and offering it to her. Finally letting go of Cyprus, she lifted up on tiptoes, and pressed a kiss against his lips. Just a quick one, she didn't want to detract from what they were doing here. But kissing him hello did seem right.

Damn, she was losing herself to these men. Not even slowly, but definitely surely.

"We need to sort this out," she said firmly as both Drey and Cyprus pulled up their own chairs. "Do we know what the other treaties say?" she asked Fane, who shook his head.

"Drey said there were five?" She nodded in response to his question. "I've only delivered two, and know about the additional one signing away your powers."

"The one from before I was born?"

"That's the one. For some reason, that one's in the public domain." Fane was almost too business like in his demeanor, and Aledwen wasn't completely sure she liked it. But then again, this was a serious subject, it was probably right he wasn't fawning over her. Though looking her in the eye might have been good. She'd have to ask about that later.

"What does it say?"

"Just what we talked about before."

"So nothing about about why my mother signed away my powers."

"I'm sorry, Aledwen," he said softly, his eyes meeting hers for a moment, before flitting away again. There was something else going on here, something about *why* he wouldn't look her in the eyes. It was odd to say the least.

"No need to be sorry. I guess we just need to work out reasons why she could want that." She jumped to her feet and began pacing back and forth in front of the fire. "What could the elvish High Lord have to offer her?" she mused aloud.

"Money?" Drey suggested.

Fane shook his head vigorously. "Elves used to be rich, but not anymore. If I was my- the High Lord, and someone was signing my treaties without questioning, then it'd be money I'd ask for."

"Is the no money a new thing?" Drey asked, and Fane shook his head again.

Cyprus also rose to his feet, and wandered over to a set of shelves that Aledwen was almost sure contained all the records of her family line back to the very beginning. Saying that, she'd never read any of them, it sounded far too dull and boring for her. But Cyprus appeared to have other ideas, as he pulled one of the books off it's shelf, and began to leaf through it.

Aledwen left him to it. There must be a reason for what he was up to, and while she was eager to know what he was thinking, she didn't want to break his train of thought.

"So it's not money the elves have that my mother wants. What magic are you good at?" She winced even as she finished asking. It was rude to inquire into another paranormal's powers. But in this case, it needed to be done.

"Not much really. We're good at fading into the background, but then so do dryads. Only difference is, we can extend that to other objects too."

"Hmm. Anything else?" After all, what did her mother have to hide? Other than the treaties themselves that was. Though signing a treaty to hide a treaty sounded ridiculous to say the least.

"I guess we're graceful, and a lot of us have healing magic." Fane frowned deeply. "I really don't understand what we have to offer the Spring Fae."

"No," Aledwen answered bluntly. There wasn't time for beating around the bush after all. But he was right. Most Spring Fae already had the ability to heal. They wouldn't, and shouldn't, need elvish magic for that. Especially not her mother, who as Queen, had more magic than most.

"I think it is masking," Cyprus said, causing all three of them to look up sharply. She was surprised, and a little disappointed that he'd spoken in front of the other two, but the apologetic look on his face, and the severity of the situation, convinced her it was necessary.

"What makes you say that?"

"Does this look a lot like you?" Cyprus placed the book he was reading down on the table, and the two other men leaned over alongside Aledwen.

"No." The woman in the picture had flaming red hair, freckles and green eyes. The latter being the only feature she and Aledwen seemed to share.

"Turn the page," Cyprus instructed.

She did so, revealing a similar picture of a small child with the same flaming red hair, with the label *Calla*.

"That's my mother's name."

"But not your mother?" he prompted. Aledwen shook her head. There was no way the child in this picture turned into her mother. "Are you sure?"

"It seems highly unlikely," she said uneasily, despite knowing her mother and this little girl shared a name.

"Turn the page again," he said.

She sucked in a breath as the next image was revealed. This time, the drawing *was* of her mother.

There was absolutely no doubt of that. But that's what didn't make any sense to Aledwen at all. Her mother didn't have red hair, or a heart shaped face, or...

"I don't think I understand."

"Or you don't want to?" Cyprus said softly, moving around so he could place his hands on her shoulder. The gesture was far more reassuring that she expected, and she leaned back into him, accepting the love and support he was giving. No. Not love. She had to stop her heart getting ahead of her, or she was going to end up in their thrall before she could even establish herself.

"Probably that."

"Will someone explain?" Drey asked, looking thoroughly confused. Fane, on the other hand, had a look of understanding on his face. It had hit him at the same time it had her.

"Aledwen's mother isn't the real Queen," he explained to the dragon. "She's using elvish masking magic to hide something big. Probably the whereabouts of the actual royal family."

"Meaning I'm not actually a princess." Aledwen's shoulders slumped, and she had to bite back the tears that were forming. She hadn't quite realised how much she liked and wanted to be royal until that moment.

"Is that a bad thing?" Drey asked softly. "More time to do the things you want if you're not."

"But also less of a chance to make a difference," she threw back instantly. It was the one thing that got her through each and every day. Once she was Queen, she *could* make a difference in the world, even if it was just to a handful of fae. Then again, once she was Queen, she'd probably have something to do with the Councils too, and the influence they had over the paranormal world.

"If it's important to you, we'll find a way to make sure you still can," Drey said. Both Fane and Cyprus nodded.

Aledwen looked in the elf's direction and raised an eyebrow, choosing not to ignore the fact he'd responded to a statement that made it sound like he too was hers.

Part of her hoped so, but he instantly averted his eyes again, which suggested he wasn't quite there yet. That was okay. She'd convince him once all this was done, and her mother was....well, she didn't know what she wanted her mother to be. Done with all the lying and the cheating and the taking stupid risks. That seemed like a reasonable request, even if she didn't think so.

"How do we find out what really happened?"

"We keep digging," Fane replied.

"We ask your mother," Drey said seconds later.

"I hardly think she's going to tell us, she didn't even want to admit that the treaties existed until I told her I knew about them," Aledwen pointed out, anger rising up within her. She hated that her mother had been so careless. But the fact her mother had lied to her...that was beyond infuriating. What had she ever done to deserve that? She'd been a good daughter, doing everything her mother wanted her to. Including staying away and out of politics. And despite that being her one true passion and something she longed to do more of.

"I can shift and we can ask. She seemed scared enough of Brandon."

"No. You are not scaring my mother into an answer. That is *not* the way we're going to do things."

"Then what do you suggest, princess?" Fane asked softly. "Your other option is to ask your mother publicly, in a way she can't deny."

"Why can't we do that?" Cyprus asked, walking around to take a seat, and trailing his hand along Aledwen's back. Goosebumps followed his touch, and thoughts she shouldn't be thinking assailed her.

"She'd probably just order our heads struck off," Fane murmured.

"She's the Queen of Spring, not the Queen of Hearts," Aledwen joked. "But actually..."

"We can use the right of becoming your life partner?" Drey suggested.

"I don't see why not," Aledwen replied, thinking deeply. It was something she'd read about once, but dismissed as never likely to be useful. She'd always found it odd that a matriarchal society had a rule that allowed male mates to demand answers of their intended's parents. But ultimately, the odd ruling worked in their favour, so she wasn't about to question it now.

"Any one of us could do it," Drey added.

"Not me-" Fane started, only to be cut off with a sharp look from the dragon.

That was odd. Her reaction to Drey's words had been instant agreement, yet Fane wasn't going with it. She wondered what all that was about. She didn't feel a pull towards him like she was between the other two in the room. But did that really mean anything?

"I can do it," Drey offered. "Maybe the fact I could eat her in one go will help."

"Don't make me repeat it again. No eating my mother. Not unless you want to find yourself in the dungeon."

"The fun dungeon?" Drey perked up.

A sly smile lifted Aledwen's lips. Now that could be fun.

"No, not the fun dungeon. The very real, very dark dungeon we have beneath the palace," she teased, while also being a little serious. No matter what her mother had done, she didn't want her to be eaten. It would cause all kinds of mess. And not just the kind which could be cleaned up with a mop.

"Alright, fine, no eating family members."

"Thank you."

"But we do need a plan," he pointed out.

"She'll hold court tomorrow. We wait until it's in full swing, then you come in asking your questions. She can't really deny your request with so many other people around."

"You're sure?" He looked uneasy, and Aledwen had to agree that it was odd.

"No, but this is our best short without threats and actual harm. So that's what I'm okay with for now."

He nodded once. "Very well." He rose from his seat, pausing where Aledwen was standing. Leaning down, he kissed her softly. "Have a good evening, Dwen."

"Wait, where are you going?" She didn't like the idea

of him leaving her, not with such an important even tomorrow.

"To relieve Brandon, so he can get some...rest." The pause in his words had her thinking of things that definitely weren't restful.

"Thank you," Cyprus answered for her, and Aledwen frowned. Now what was all that about.

"I'd better go too," Fane jumped to his feet. "Good night, princess."

He rushed past them all, and Drey looked on in bemusement. "He'll realise eventually." He cracked a smile. "Have fun without me." With that, he followed the elf from the room.

"So...which way to your room?" Cyprus murmured as he stepped up to her, and wrapped his arms around her waist, pulling her back into him.

"This way," she said a little breathlessly, pulling his arms away, but grabbing his hand to tug him along behind her.

FIFTEEN

She wasn't as nervous as when it had been her and Drey. Which pretty much meant she wasn't nervous at all. There was something about all of the men that had suddenly appeared in her life, that had her feeling safe and secure. More than she had in her entire life. If this was what finding a mate, or in her case, mates, was like, then no longer was it mythical. Everyone should have this.

Aledwen reached up and touched Cyprus' face, smoothing her thumb against his cheek. His green eyes looked on with intense devotion, filling her with joy.

But he didn't let her enjoy it. Or he did, just not in the way she had been. Instead, he pressed his lips against hers, taking her in a demanding kiss and backing her against the wall behind them. Her hands grasped at his shirt, tugging at the material and desperate to remove it. He was hers, and she was desperate to feel all of him.

"Off," she moaned into the kiss, receiving a chuckle

in return. But he also played along, pulling away from their kiss, and quickly divesting himself of the shirt, letting the starched white material fall to the floor.

He kissed her again, and she wished more than anything that she was a witch, and that she could magically divest them of all their clothing, but as that wasn't going to happen, she'd have to break the mood by trying to get off the terrible contraption she was wearing.

"Can you rip it?" she asked, only pausing their kiss for a moment. She didn't want the contact to be lost for long.

"Yes," he responded breathlessly, and she felt a sharpened claw down her back, splitting the fabric as it did, but not her skin. Cyprus was too careful for that. For which she was grateful, even if it wouldn't have mattered in her current state.

He tugged at the sleeves of her dress, and she shrugged out of it in an attempt to help him. Soon, it joined his shirt on the floor.

One more horrible dress ruined. Just a whole wardrobe left to go.

Her naked skin pressed against his, and the heat grew within her. She pressed her body against his, whimpering softly as she felt him press into her. He was still wearing too many clothes. Why was he wearing any clothes at all?

Aledwen slipped her hands between them and swiftly divested him of the rest, leaving him bare and ready to take her.

She took him in her hand, moving it up and down. This angle wouldn't do though. She wasn't short, but she was shorter than him, and backed against a wall just wasn't going to work.

Without breaking their kiss, she'd already had to do that too much, she jumped up slightly, letting go of him and wrapping her arms around his neck. Her legs crossed behind his back, pulling him closer to her.

Cyprus steadied her with one arm under her ass, and the other hand pressed against the wall. Aledwen moaned. The next part couldn't come fast enough.

With him otherwise occupied, she reached down again, ensuring her other arm kept tight hold of his neck, and guided him to her. Cyprus took over then, thrusting into her, and seating himself so she tipped her head back, finally ending their kiss. It didn't matter though, not with his lips moving down her neck, nibbling and sucking on the sensitive skin there.

"I see you started without me, brother," Brandon's amused voice came from the door.

Aledwen's eyes opened, and she looked in his direction, unsurprised to see his hooded stare watching them intently. Cyprus didn't respond at all, unless she counted the extra powerful thrust that pulled more whimpers and moans from her.

Brandon licked his lips. "How do you feel about me joining, Dwen?" he asked her. All she could do in response was nod. "I was hoping you'd say that."

He quickly stripped himself, leaving him as naked as the two of them were. And for the same reason. Excitement flowed through her, and she was sure Cyprus could feel her reaction from where he was inside her.

"I'm going to move you to the bed," Cyprus panted, and she nodded eagerly. Anything that got the two both moving against her. In her.

Where were these thoughts even coming from? She'd never been this way inclined before. But with them, this new direction was exciting.

Cyprus held her tight as he walked her over to the bed, withdrawing from her as he dropped her there.

"How do you want to do this?" Cyprus asked his brother, who gave a contented smile that had very little to do with sex. In fact, she suspected it was more to do with Cyprus talking aloud. Saying that, she was sure their ability to communicate wordlessly was going to be a great advantage for her.

"Let's just go with it," Brandon replied, his smile changing from contented, to a lot more conniving. So long as he had good things planned for her, she didn't mind.

Brandon moved over and sat on the bed next to her, making her move so she was perched next to him. Without waiting for either of the twins to make a move, she pressed her body against Brandon's and gave him a searing kiss. Maybe this shouldn't have been the way they'd had their first one, but she couldn't really bring herself to care.

He returned it instantly, and pulled her closer to him, leading Aledwen to straddle him. His hands roamed her body, each touch burning in its intensity. She wanted him, so badly. Just as much as she wanted his twin, who she could feel watching. She hoped he was touching himself too. At the sight of her, pressed against his brother, with the clear intention of doing far more than that.

Not wanting to wait any longer, Aledwen positioned herself over Brandon. He helped her guide him, and the moment he entered, her head dipped forward, and she had to refrain from screaming. He was similar to his brother, but she was already so sensitive from having Cyprus inside her anyway.

Brandon set a smooth easy rhythm, and she fell into it easily. After a few moments, he leaned backwards, lying back on the bed, and taking Aledwen with him, so her ass was in the air and presented towards Cyprus. She hadn't thought she could get more turned on, but the idea of what he could do with that...

"Cyprus..." she moaned, almost begging, but not quite able to.

"Are you sure?" he asked, placing a hand on her back and drawing circles against her skin.

"Yes." She nodded furiously.

"She wants it, brother," Brandon said through baited breath. "Who are we to say no."

To her surprise, Cyprus laughed slightly.

Brandon pulled out of her, making Aledwen whimper. Why had he ended things, it was just getting to the good bit.

"Don't worry, Dwen. we just need to make sure you're ready." His hands trailed down and cupped her breasts, before taking each of her nipples in turn and squeezing them tightly.

As he did, Cyprus dipped his fingers inside her, making her wiggle and moan. After a few moments, he drew her wetness back and used it somewhere else.

Dark pleasure filled her. She'd never done this before. She'd never wanted to, but right now, not even a disaster could stop her from wanting to.

The wait was excruciating, and only serving to turn her on more. Gently, Brandon entered her again, leaving her feeling very full, and wondering how Cyprus was going to fit.

He pressed against her ass, and she tensed up on reflex.

"Relax," he said softly. "We don't have to do this if you don't want."

"I want it," she panted.

"Just relax then."

She did her best, but at first it hurt, until it didn't. She was full. Very full, but feeling the twins both within her went beyond anything she'd experienced before. And when they each bit into one of her shoulders, sealing the bond they'd started, she felt far more completed than she ever had before.

And yet there was still a piece of her missing.

SIXTEEN

Waking with an auburn haired twin on each side of her was bliss. More so because they'd both been touching her still, and because they'd instigated more as they'd woken up...

Aledwen pushed the thoughts away. Now really wasn't the time for them. She needed to get ready for her mother holding court. Which meant choosing exactly the right thing to wear. Normally, she'd just go for comfort, but today was too important for that. Really, she needed to look like a Queen. Or at least, someone who could pass as a Queen. That was the only way she was actually going to win over the fae themselves.

They probably didn't care one way or another if wrongdoing had happened. But then, she didn't know any of them well enough to know for sure. Maybe *all* they cared about was right and wrong. Though that did seem a little unlikely. Stability was likely their main goal. Hence her need to look like a Queen today.

And she wanted her men to see her looking good, and like she was in charge of the room. Not of them, well, yes of them, but her power was important.

Wow, she sounded conceited. But it was true. She wasn't coming into their relationships as the underdog. She had a position of power in her own right.

She selected a sleek gown of a soft grey colour. It was understated and at least a little elegant. Plus, she had a circlet that would match perfectly. Anything to remind the other fae she was their princess. And she needed that. Most of them wouldn't recognise her as a person after all.

Luckily, this dress was easy for her to put on, so she didn't need to call for help. Which was always a good thing. She always felt unbelievably helpless when people had to help her dress. That was one of the downsides of being royalty. If she didn't want to make a difference so badly, then she'd give it all up in an instant.

"Knock, knock." Drey's voice was followed by two sharp taps on her door.

She smiled to herself, amused by his clear attempt at not being private. It was a good job she'd just zipped up her dress, and that there was no one outside the door who hadn't already seen her naked.

Her cheeks heated at that thought.

"Morning," she said, looking away and back into the mirror to fix her hair. It was shining in the sunlight streaming through her window, and she felt better than she had...ever. Clearly the previous night had made a difference to her. A good difference. Though the feeling was slightly odd given that she hadn't known she needed to change anything.

"Did you have a good night?"

"Yes, thank you." She blushed. There was no way he didn't know what she'd done the night before. Glancing over her shoulder, one look at his face told her that he not only knew, but was enjoying the image.

Drey closed the gap between them. Dropping a kiss on the top of her head, before leaning in close so she could feel his hot breath against her ear. "Maybe I could watch sometime."

"No," she replied instantly. "It's for the twins and I. Like our time is for us." She twisted around to place a gentle kiss against his lips, trying to convey that she wasn't being cruel. She just felt that their relationships should be kept separate for now.

"Okay then," he chirped, surprisingly cheery. "Are you ready to go to court?"

"Almost, just let me fix my hair." She turned back the mirror and ran her head through the light brown strands. She should leave it loose. It'd be more practical tied back, she supposed, though she did love the way it felt around her shoulders.

Picking up the circlet, she fixed it atop of her head, ensuring that the dark pearl dangling from the middle of the bright silver, was in the centre of her forehead. There'd be nothing worse than having an off centre head piece.

She rose to her feet, and held her arm out to Drey, thankful that he took it instantly. "Now, I'm ready," she said, holding her head high and trying to channel the confidence she was only half feeling.

"You look beautiful," Drey said.

"Thank you."

"And very much like a Queen."

"Perfect."

He led her out of her room, and down through the halls she knew so well.

"Where is everyone?" he asked after a few moments.

"At court, I assume," Aledwen answered.

"But..."

"Haven't you heard of being fashionably late?"

"Well, yes, but..."

"And making an entrance?" she teased, a smirk lifting her mouth.

"Oh."

"Yes. Maximum impact." She'd never felt more devious than she did right now, but it'd be worth it. When she entered her mother's throne room, all eyes were going to be on her. And they were going to have to listen to what she had to say.

SEVENTEEN

T he guard outside the door looked particularly
uneasy when Aledwen asked her to announce her.
Not that anyone would blame her. She was being faced
off by a rather determined looking princess with a dragon
shifter on her arm. That was intimidating enough,
without knowing that what was about to happen would
go against the Queen's wishes.

"Announcing her Royal Highness, Fae Princess of
Spring, Aledwen, and her escort, Dreyfus of Flock
Kinnon." The woman's voice cracked with nerves, but
Aledwen was pleased. She'd already opened the door and
announced them after all. The damage was done
whether she wanted it to be or not.

A hush fell over the room as Aledwen and Drey
stepped in. She tamped down on the urge to grin like a
fool, and kept her face a cool mask of calm.

As she walked towards the throne at the back of the
room, she was unsurprised to find the twins standing

sentry over her mother. She nodded at each of them, a gesture they returned. Which was helpful. Not having to voice things to them would allow this to run much more smoothly.

"Good morning." Aledwen kept her voice steady, ensuring it carried throughout the room for everyone to hear. There was no point wrestling away power, if not everyone was able to witness it. "I'd like to introduce my mates to the court."

There was a murmur throughout the room, though whether it was because of what she was doing, or her use of the plural mates, she wasn't sure.

"Daughter," her mother acknowledged. There was a slight shake in her voice that told Aledwen all she needed to know. Her mother knew what was coming, or at the very least suspected. She hoped it wasn't one of the men who'd told her. But she doubted it. She'd seen how angry they'd been.

Aledwen let go of Drey's arm, and took her seat on the throne one step down from her mother's. She wasn't quite sure what had happened to her, but she was suddenly particularly resentful about the way her mother had treated her throughout her life.

Just why had she been hidden away. Well, not hidden away as such. But why hadn't she been part of society like any good heir should be? It was like her mother had waited until the last possible moment to let her know the other fae. It had to be about keeping hold of her power, and if their theory was correct, then there was a very good reason…

"Are you going to introduce us?" her mother hissed from the side of her mouth, but Aledwen didn't fail to notice the worried sidelong glance she gave Cyprus, who was to Aledwen's right, as she spoke.

"Everyone, it is my pleasure to announce, Dreyfus of Flock Kinnon, and Brandon and Cyprus Reed," she nodded towards each of them as she said their names, and they each turned to bow to her in turn. Drey had told her that would happen. Apparently he'd spent some time reading while he'd been guarding her mother, and found it was common practice for a fae's fated mate.

"Welcome to the Spring Court," the Queen said through gritted teeth. "Do any of you wish to address the court?" This time, her voice shook, and Aledwen almost felt a perverse sense of pleasure over the fact her mother was on such a back foot. It had taken a long time to get her to this stage.

"I do," Drey responded instantly, taking a step towards them. He gave Aledwen a lingering look, before shifting his attention to the older woman.

"As Aledwen's mate, I wish to know if there are any outstanding marriage requests."

The Queen's face blanched as clear panic overtook her. There was no way she could lie here. Getting caught out in a lie would be particularly bad for her right now.

"There is a treaty that hasn't been signed yet, requesting Aledwen's hand in marriage, yes."

"And does this treaty pertain to anything else?" he asked, his dark eyes narrowed towards the throne. If it was Aledwen under his gaze, then she'd have been scared beyond belief. Then again, if it was her he was looking at, then his expression would be much, much different.

"Yes," her mother admitted quietly.

"Care to elaborate?" His voice was almost as cold as Aledwen's emotions, and she didn't blame him. The moment the two of them, or more accurately, the four of them, let their emotions get the better of them, was the moment they lost control of the situation. Which was already proving difficult enough from Brandon's balled fists at the other side of the throne.

Aledwen longed to go comfort him, to let him know that it was all going to be alright. But that wouldn't help their cause.

"There's a series of treaties between the elvish High Lord and I."

"I can corroborate." Fane stepped forward from the rest of the assembled court. His gaze flickered to Aledwen, before turning away again. She had no idea what was going on there. But a tug in her gut told her that he was as much hers as the rest of them were.

Only he didn't seem to feel the same.

"Please go on," Drey prompted, though she knew it was all for show.

"What do you want me to say?" Her mother's anger rose, and Aledwen bit back a smile. While the Queen may not realise it, she was doing exactly what they wanted her to. If she was angry, then she'd likely let things slip that she shouldn't otherwise. Which pretty much the only way they were going to be able to catch her out.

If Cyprus' theory was true, then there was no doubt of her mother's intelligence. She just hoped they hadn't underestimated her. That would end badly. Probably with a trip down to the dungeons and an appointment with some chains. Her mother would stay clear of torture at least.

And that was why she'd kept Aledwen away from the rest of the fae. If she ever caused a problem, then she'd be easy to get rid of because no one knew, or cared about her. What her mother probably hadn't expected, was for her to end up with three shifters in tow. Or an elf.

No. She couldn't think of Fane like that. Not yet anyway. He clearly hadn't accepted what he was to her yet. Even if the other three had already recognised. Meaning Fane probably knew already, just wasn't acting on it, bizarrely.

"Please tell us about your treaties."

"There isn't much to tell."

"What's in them?" Drey asked, his piercing eyes never leaving her.

"That is none of your business," her mother half-shouted. Perfect, she was just where they needed her.

"As one of the future Consorts of Spring, I think it is." Drey kept surprisingly calm, showing neither his anger nor his excitement.

"You know what's in them."

"Better than you do, I expect," Drey announced loudly, causing a cascade of gasps throughout the room.

"That's-"

"Completely true," Fane broke in. "I've brought all of

the treaties since the Princess Aledwen's birth, and
you've signed all but the most recent one without even
asking to read it. No fae has even been remotely interested until the Princess was allowed to court." His eyes
flickered to her again, and this time there was no
mistaking the protectiveness and affection that was
lingering there. He was definitely as much a part of her as
the others. His speaking out for her now was a good indication of that.

"That doesn't mean-" her mother started.

"You could have signed away anything," Drey
pointed out.

"You almost signed away your own daughter," Fane
added, receiving a sharp look from the dragon. He hadn't
intended for that information to come from anyone other
than the Queen herself.

However, it still seemed to have the desired effect,
and the assembled fae began to titter among themselves.

Deciding enough was enough, Aledwen rose to her
feet, straightening her spine and trying to sound as confi-
dent as possible. Which would be hard, considering she
was shaking inside. This wasn't quite what she imagined
would happen when she was finally allowed at court.

"What did you gain from the first treaty, Your
Majesty?" she asked coldly. Her mother looked her way,
with fear in her eyes. But this wasn't fear of Aledwen.
Nor was it fear of losing her. Instead, it appeared to be
the fear of getting caught. Which worried her no end.
And broke her heart more than a little.

That look told her all she needed to know. Her

mother had never truly cared for her. Even the small acts of affection she'd felt over the years had just been acts to try and control her. All Aledwen represented to her mother was a loss of power. Especially now she was eighteen and would take over the Birth.

"Well?" Drey prompted, but Aledwen waved him down. This was on her now. She needed to show the fae who she really was.

"Masking powers," her mother whispered.

"Masking powers for what?" Aledwen asked loudly, making sure that the court could actually hear.

"To hide the truth."

"What truth?" Aledwen pressed.

"That I killed the previous princess," her mother shouted.

Shock rippled through the room, and even Aledwen was taken aback. That hadn't been what she'd expected her mother to admit. At least not so easily, and not quite so brutally. In her imagination, the worst they were going to have to deal with was power stripping. This was just a completely different level.

"Leave us," she ordered the fae, her voice scarily commanding even to herself. "And send in some of the guards."

The fae were quick to leave and she wasn't surprised. They probably didn't want to be around for the drama that was about to happen. She didn't really want to be either. But this was her job now.

"How did you kill her?" Aledwen's voice shook. How could it not? She was inquiring after someone's *death*.

"It was an accident..."

"Tell us," she ordered.

Slowly, she watched the Queen crumple in on herself as the words sprung forth. A hunting accident is what it sounded like, though there was no real way of verifying that. Cold fury settled in Aledwen as the whole story unfolded. Basically, they'd covered the whole thing up. Anyone who was around at the same time as the flame haired princess still saw her when they looked at the current Queen.

"And you hid me away because..."

"No one would have believed you were from the same line."

"How could you do that to a child?" Brandon half-shouted.

"I had no choice. It was that, or let the world know what had happened."

"Why didn't you just explain?" Aledwen asked. "What's the worst that could happen?"

"I could have been killed," her mother spat out.

"So you decided to pretend to be Queen instead?"

"No. I pretended to be the princess. When my eighteenth birthday came, the true powers transferred to me, and I became the princess in truth and not just in name." Anger seeped through every word, but Aledwen was having none of this. There had been decades in which her mother could have come clean, and yet she never had. That was more telling than anything.

"So where does that leave us? You're the proper

Queen now, and I'm what?" She was genuinely curious, and genuinely a little concerned.

"You're still the princess if that's what you want to know. The powers are ours. Is that really all you care about?" Her mother's disgust flowed through her.

"No. I care about our people, and not *lying* to them. If there's another person waiting to take my place, then I want to know something about it. That way, I can actually have a civil conversation before they end up thinking I stole their powers, like you stole their mother's." She'd never been so angry in her life, and something unfamiliar bubbled under the surface. Maybe she was finally getting the magic she so needed. They did say that the truth set people free.

"There is no one else. And if you think you're ready for this..." her mother snarled, but backed off quickly when Drey hissed, and the twins glared at her with narrowed eyes.

"No, I'm not ready for this. I've never had an opportunity to get to know our people, or learn about my position or my magic, but I'll do a damned sight better than lying to them for decades."

"You think it's so easy..." her mother started again.

"Guards, please place her under house arrest. In her quarters please, and still deliver the necessary comforts. I'll let the people decide what to do with her." Her voice held strong, surprising her. She almost didn't expect that to be the case. There was so much going on in her head after all.

The four guards in the room nodded, and did exactly

as she bid, receiving a surprisingly small amount of resistance from her mother. While they'd started getting things sorted out, Aledwen was well aware there was more to do than just putting her away.

"Are you okay?" Cyprus asked softly, once the room had been vacated by all except her and the four men.

She nodded, looking between them, and noticing Fane's discomfort. She didn't know what was going on there. But she'd need to find out soon.

EIGHTEEN

"Guess I should try the stone again," Aledwen said once she'd calmed down a little. And she did mean a little. She was definitely still on edge from everything, and even more so because whether or not her magic would work now, could end up making all the difference.

Slowly, she approached the stone, the guys, including Fane, trailing along behind her. She braced herself as she placed her hands on it, drawing the magic from within it. This time, something battered against her skin, wanting out. It was almost like what she'd felt earlier, but not quite.

The stone reflected that. It sparked green in places, just like it had when it was just her and Drey, though this time, it was sparking a little bit brighter. Because of the twins? That seemed likely. Which meant she was probably right about the real link between her and Fane. Now all she had to do was get him to see that too.

Aledwen let go of the stone, and the little lights faded to nothing.

"Fane?"

"Yes, Your Majesty."

"Is there a reason you're not acting on the mating bond between us?" she asked outright, trying to meet his eyes, but failing. Mostly because of him. The elf was still doing everything possible to avoid looking at her. There was definitely something else going on.

"I don't know what you mean."

"Really?" Drey interrupted. "Then why are you refusing to look at her?" He sounded amused, and Aledwen held back a smile. Drey would definitely be an asset if she just needed someone to come out and say something. Though maybe not if tact and diplomacy needed to be engaged. She wondered if dragons were all like that. It could explain why the dragon wars were happening still. That was still perfectly ridiculous in her eyes.

"I shouldn't be looking at what isn't mine," he answered instantly, drawing a barking laugh from Brandon.

"That's an archaic rule, Fane. It's not going to wash with me. Now, tell me the real reason."

"I can't, Dwen."

His use of her shortened name shocked her a moment. The only people who'd ever thought to use it were in this room, and it was odd hearing it from someone who always came across so formal.

"Leave, please," Aledwen told the others.

They each kissed her on the cheek as they left and she caught herself smiling. She could definitely get used to the amount of small indications of love and affection. It was kind of a lot to take in compared to how little she'd received up until now. But that didn't matter. Deep down, she knew how true their feelings were.

"You wanted to talk to me alone?" Fane asked, his voice shaking slightly.

"Yes. Will you tell me why you won't accept it now?"

"No."

"But it is there." She didn't ask. There was no question as far as she was concerned.

He stayed silent for a little too long. "No."

"Very well. Tell me about the High Lord."

"Why?" Fane frowned at her, but she ignored him, moving over to sit back on the smaller of the two thrones. She didn't sit formally though, instead, she leaned backwards, making herself comfortable.

"Just because my mother is mostly dealt with, doesn't mean the High Lord is. He's still going to pose a problem. And if what you've said is true, he still has the magic that should be a part of me. And still wants to marry me."

"I don't know what you want me to tell you." He sighed, and slumped against the wall next to the Birthing stone.

"The truth."

"He's my brother," Fane blurted out. "Telling you feels a little bit like a betrayal."

"Oh."

"Yet there's part of me that wants to. You confuse me,

Dwen. Every part of me is begging to be near you, and I want to listen, oh so badly. But my sense of duty says I can't. That betraying my people will end badly."

She stared at him, not quite sure how to process that one. Or what to do about it.

Rising from the throne, she moved towards where Fane was sitting, and slumped down next to him. There wasn't much space between them, but she was respectful in leaving a small gap, even if she didn't want to.

"Can elves really deny a mating bond?" she asked, genuinely curious if that was the case.

"Yes. It's one of the few powers we have. But..." he trailed off, the hand she could see shaking. Without thinking about whether it was a good idea or not, she leaned over and placed one of her hands over it.

"But?"

"It hurts. I'm really feeling it. My body wants me to get further away from you, or to give in to it."

"And you're still going with the former option?" She sighed. While the last thing she wanted to do was push him into something he wasn't ready for, she was also dimly aware that their bond remaining unsealed was likely the reason her magic wasn't working.

"Yes."

"Even though that's what keeps my magic locked away?" She wished she hadn't just thought about it, then the words might not have slipped out. But even so, the words needed to be said.

"You want me to choose between my loyalty to you,

and my loyalty to my brother?" he asked, shock covering his features.

"Of course not. I'm sorry, please forget I said that."

"Doesn't make it less true though."

"No." Tears pooled in the corners of her eyes, and she swiped them away. Now wasn't the time for them.

"I'm sorry, Dwen."

To her surprise, he leaned over, and cupped her cheek in his hands, smoothing his thumb across her skin. The tension built between them, and she wanted more than anything to kiss him. But unlike with the others, she knew that he needed to come to her. Especially if it accidentally sealed the bond he wasn't on board with. That wasn't how she wanted to win her final mate.

How she knew he was the last one, she wasn't sure, but there was a point in time where trusting her instincts seemed to be the good way to go.

Tentatively, he pressed his lips against hers, kissing her softly. It was tender, undemanding, and the promise of many more kisses to come.

Except that it wasn't. Aledwen pulled away, knowing this wasn't what he actually wanted.

"We need to stop," she whispered. "I take it a kiss doesn't seal anything for you?" Her voice cracked, and she almost regretted it. But showing her vulnerability seemed safe.

"Not unless I want it to," he said sadly.

"I know you're not ready to do anything about it, but I'm here when you change your mind," she told him, cupping his cheek and staring into his eyes. She could get lost there. The intelligence, the depth of the feeling, and the trust there was unbelievable. She just wished he'd give in to her, but could understand why he wouldn't.

"Thank you," he whispered.

"Is there any way I can make it so you won't be betraying anyone?"

"Short of not being a princess anymore..." he trailed of and looked at her, his eyes widening with excitement.

"What?" She gave him a confused smile, his enthusiasm catching.

"How long have you got before the Birth."

"Two days, why?"

"Dwen, if you're not a princess anymore, then you're not bound to the treaties."

"True. But I'm not going to abdicate. All I've wanted, all my life, was to make a difference. And to do that, I need to be Queen."

"I don't need you to abdicate. I just need you to do exactly what you want to."

"You've lost me," she said with a slightly uneasy laugh.

"Become the Queen you've always wanted to be, Dwen. It solves all our problems." Fane seemed so certain that she almost believed him.

"Yes, a coronation is always the easiest option." Aledwen sighed. If only it was that easy.

"Your people won't accept your mother as Queen now. Get them to accept you, and you can be crowned. The treaty is void then anyway..."

"Are you sure that will work?" she asked, the excitement really catching now she knew what he meant.

"Yes." He leaned forward and pressed a quick kiss against her lips again. "Please, Dwen. That will solve a lot of our problems in one go."

She pondered for a moment. He wasn't actually wrong. Being crowned as Queen would stop her mother being able to wrestle back power, as well as allowing Fane to accept their mating bond. Though she wasn't naive enough to believe there'd be no other kick back from that. She was sure there'd be some. Probably from the dragons too if what Drey said about them normally only mating with other dragon shifters was true.

"Okay, let me see what I can do."

NINETEEN

Aledwen wrung her hands together. The nerves were definitely getting to her, which made no sense. She'd taken on her mother in front of the fae just this morning, and yet, now it was affecting her more. She'd even gone as far as requesting all the half-fae, and the wolf shifter protectors were in the room too. They had as much right to have a say here as anyone.

"Are you sure you're going to be okay?" Brandon asked, touching his hand to her arm and leaning in slightly.

"Yes, I'll be fine. These are my people, they won't hurt me."

"We can stay with you if you want."

"Thank you," she said, touching his face. "But you know why you can't. If they say yes, then I don't want to start my reign with them being scared of my mates. Fear isn't the way to run a court."

"You and my sister are going to get on like a house on fire." He smiled affectionately.

"I'm looking forward to meeting her properly." She wasn't even lying. Everything the twins had told her about their sister had made her more and more excited to meet the woman. Plus, she wouldn't lie, having the in to the Shifter Council would be good. It could mean that Aledwen could start making a difference in the world at large.

"Me too." He kissed her cheek. "We'll see you soon." He trailed his hand along her arm, and joined Drey and Cyprus as they left the room. Aledwen looked after them, longing shooting through her. How had she become so lucky? Just a week ago, she'd been alone and dreading the Birth. Now, she had mates around her, and was about to get the support she needed to become Queen.

Now that was a terrifying thought. Her, a Queen. At eighteen. While it had been part of the plan, it hadn't been a part of her immediate one. But she'd heard that life tended to take its own path most of the time. She just hoped she was ready for it.

"Good afternoon," she called, and the noise in the room quieted to a murmur. "First, I wish to apologise for this morning. We've since discovered the truth. The Fae Princess of Spring before my mother, died in a tragic hunting accident. My mother has been using elvish magic to hide the truth from you all."

The murmur rose until it was close to deafening. This was never going to work.

"Please," Aledwen shouted. "Please, just give me a

moment to tell you what I know, and the solution I have. I won't do anything without your permission, that's not how I want to work."

"Did you know about this?" a rather large fae called out, her long blonde hair not doing her any favours either.

"Not until last night. Something my mother said tipped me off, and with the help of the representative of House Paige, we worked out what was going on. This morning was the confrontation of my mother."

This time, the murmurs were quieter, but they only made Aledwen more nervous. She really wasn't sure how to take any of this. Were they okay with her? Or did they hate her as a result of what her mother had done?

"I've been hidden away for eighteen years so no one would notice my hair colour. But now it's too late, and I'm needed to perform the Birth." Aledwen took a deep breath, feeling a little bit calmer now she knew she was right. There really wasn't any choice in any of this. For them or for her.

"But what does that mean now?" someone asked.

This was it. the moment she had to put forth the one idea that may not go down very well.

"My mother signed away the magic of Spring," she announced to the room, holding her hands out in an attempt to calm the outrage she knew there'd be. "And there's only one way to get it back. According to the latest treaty, I need to marry the elvish High Lord. But that's where the problems start."

The room had gone completely silent now. Which surprised her. She hadn't realised she'd be such a good public speaker. Though admittedly, she'd never had a reason to try.

"I'm already mated. And that marriage would break the sacred bond I have with those men." A lot of the fae looked around the room, probably trying to spot Drey and the twins. "They're not in the room, we felt that would be unfair on you all with the decision I'm going to ask you to make."

"And what is that?" one of the half-fae asked.

"If I'm not a princess, then the treaty is null and void. My fourth mate can unlock my magic, and I can perform the Birth as I'm supposed to do. And no, we've already checked, there isn't any other option. The previous royal line died out when my mother took over." The last words tasted bitter, but she knew she had to say them. Otherwise the fae would never go for it.

"Queen Calla should not be replaced!" One of the wolf-shifters pushed to the front, glaring at her angrily. She recognised him instantly. He was the same wolf who'd faced off against her the other day over Drey. She'd known he'd be a problem, but was surprised how quickly that had actually come to pass.

"What choice do we have?" one of the fae asked him. "The princess is the only member of the royal family we have. If the spring doesn't come..."

"And you want someone leading you who has mates that aren't-"

"That aren't what?" Aledwen demanded of the wolf shifter. "There are no male fae anyway, meaning it can't be that. And it doesn't matter anyway because *I* don't get a say in it. We all know how mating works. It's a case of fate deciding and us just having to go with it. And I think you'll find that having the mates I do, will only make me a stronger ruler."

She saw a lot of nodding heads, and relief flooded through her. She didn't really want to go against their wishes if she couldn't help it. But if the Birth was delayed, then the consequences could be dire. And she wasn't willing to let her mother out of the dungeon to do it in her stead.

"I need your permission to hold a coronation," Aledwen said loudly. "It'll have to be tomorrow, so we're still ready for the birth. But I refuse to start my possible reign without the support of my people. But please know, I'll always hold your best interests at heart."

She knew they had no reason to actually believe her, and that really, their hands were being forced by the lack of leader, and the upcoming Birth. But given time, she'd prove herself again and again to them until they believed her.

"All in favour of the Princess Aledwen's motion?" the court announcer called.

To Aledwen's supreme relief, most of the hands in the room were raised. They wanted her. They were willing to crown her and let her lead them.

TWENTY

The aisle towards the throne seemed to be ten times longer than it ever had before. Especially with the Birthing stone sat to the back, taunting her. If this all went wrong, then she'd never have any reason to use it. And they'd have big problems on their hands. Unless the weather on Earth had managed to set itself into a proper pattern without the fae's interference. But she doubted it.

Drey and the twins waited at the front for her, in their rightful place as consorts. Fane was at the back somewhere. She could feel his eyes on her. But while he wasn't a formally introduced mate of hers, he couldn't stand there. He also didn't want to provoke any other issues, which could happen if his brother became aware of the situation.

Then again, things had moved so quickly that even Aledwen wasn't too sure what was happening, so she'd be surprised if anyone else outside the tight circle of the Spring Fae would.

Once she was crowned, she'd have to make herself known to the other fae Queens. A formal introduction so to speak. Which could be interesting since she hadn't had anything to do with them ever.

Aledwen vowed that her own daughter would never be in this situation. She'd be ready for the day she became Queen. Not just because she'd know her people, but also because she'd know the other players in the game.

Of course, her daughter would also have the advantage of not having her magic signed away before she was born. That was always a good start.

She glided forward, all her concentration on keeping the ornate robes she was wearing straight. She wished she'd never complained about how uncomfortable her formal dresses were, because this truly took the cake. It was heavy, and stiflingly warm. She actively had to try not think about how much she was sweating. A shower would definitely be in order before any fun time with her mates.

Well, with Fane. That's what she hoped would be happening after this ceremony ended. The other fae would be having a ball, but quite frankly, she'd had enough of those. How they dealt with one a night in the lead up to the Birth was beyond her. Maybe she'd understand when she had a few years experience.

Reaching the end of the aisle, she knelt, bowing her head before the Master of Ceremonies. It seemed a little anticlimactic that he was the one crowning her, but it did sort of make sense. The approval she needed was of the weather, the magic, and the fae themselves. Not from any religion or higher power.

"Fae Princess of Spring, we transform you. No longer will you solely be the vessel for the Birth, but the channel for all of Spring," the Master of Ceremonies said.

Because that wasn't slightly terrifying. And a lot of pressure. How was she going to live up to all of that?

Oh well, problems for another day, she guessed.

A wave of energy passed through her, though as before, she wasn't able to actually access it. Probably to do with the pool of magic the Elvish High Lord was keeping from her. She just had to hope he didn't notice it had grown before she could seal her bond with Fane. Or if he did, that he couldn't do anything about it fast enough.

Though what could he do? Pitchforks at the gate seemed unlikely. People would notice that. And stand up for that.

Which was when she realised she had no idea where the elves even lived. She'd have to ask Fane. Maybe he'd even take her there one day. When everything had calmed down a little bit, obviously.

"And so it be done. Rise, Fae Queen of Spring."

Aledwen carefully rose to her feet, pulling robes out of the way of her feet as she did. Tripping over them wouldn't be a great look for her. Not in the slightest.

Cheers came from the assembled fae, but she didn't feel like she deserved them yet. There was so much still to do. A bond to seal, and the Birth to get through tomorrow. Then actually proving herself...maybe in another year or three she'd actually be able to enjoy the sentiment. But for now, not so much.

She turned to face everyone assembled, not allowing her gaze to linger on three of her mates. She'd talked to them earlier anyway, and they knew and understood what she needed to do right now.

Slowly, Aledwen walked back down the aisle, nodding to the various rows of assembled fae. The closer she drew to the back, the more nervous she became. There was a chance that Fane may have changed his mind. And if so, she'd asked her people to put faith in her over something she couldn't deliver.

There was also the wolf shifters to consider. The alpha of one of the packs was glaring at her. She really had made an enemy there, and she couldn't even put her finger on why. She made a note to watch him closely. And maybe to get Drey to do some digging. Or Cyprus. he was much better at being sneaky.

Drawing level with where Fane was now standing, she dipped into an awkward curtsy. Her robes definitely weren't made for this. Technically, she shouldn't be doing any kind of bowing to anyone, but offering one of her mates the same respect he showed for her, seemed like a small price to pay for them.

"Dwen," he whispered.

"You ready to take the risk?" she asked quietly, her words drowned out by the noise around them. No one could go anywhere until she left the room, but they were certainly already planning the party they were going to have.

"Absolutely."

Fane offered her his arm, and she hooked her own through it, resting her hand against the stiff fabric of his jacket. At least that would be gone soon. It wouldn't matter much for what they had planned.

While disappointed that her robes didn't allow for her to walk any faster, anticipation was already building inside Aledwen. She had some idea what this was going to be like given her experiences with her other mates. But at the same time, Fane was her fourth and her final.. It was going to be something completely different at the same time.

"This is us," she said once they reached the door of her rooms. She smiled at him, and received one in return. "I...err...hate to break the moment, but I need a bath before we..."

"Want me to run one for you while you take these off?" he asked, his eyes looking into her softly.

She nodded once, and pointed him in the right direction, before beginning to remove her robes. She just hoped she'd never have to wear them again. After wearing these, being naked for the Birth hardly seemed like an issue before. Especially not if she had the magic she should have been born with.

After folding the stiff green material of her outer robe, she began to work on the softer inner one. It was just as ornate, and just as heavy. Which was just ridiculous. No one was ever going to see it. Even now, with someone else in her rooms with her, she was the only one who could see the intricately sewn leaves and flowers.

The seamstresses had taken a very long time trying to make these robes reflect how spring looked and felt. More people should be allowed to enjoy their beauty.

Oh well, not really her problem, she supposed. She'd work on breaking traditions later.

"Your bath's ready," Fane said, walking back towards her and kissing her neck. "Am I okay to join you?" he whispered in her ear.

Aledwen nodded swiftly, twisting around so she could look at him. "I'd like that."

He took her hands in his, and drew her towards the bathroom. With gentle fingers, he brushed her long brown hair behind her ear, before moving down and pushing the strap of her under-dress from her shoulder. It slipped to the floor with a gentle flutter, and she had to swallow the lump that formed in her throat.

"Get into the water, Dwen. I can feel how tense you are."

She nodded, doing as he suggested, but not taking her eyes off him as he stripped off his clothing. There was something mesmerising about his movements, and she almost didn't want him to stop. Except that would mean he wouldn't get into the water with her.

After what seemed like an age, he did. Sinking beneath the water, and leaning in towards her. Aledwen rested her head on his shoulder, loving the comfort he was offering more than anyone could possibly imagine.

"You ready to seal the bond?" he asked.

She nodded, closing her eyes very briefly. "How do you want to do it?" she asked him.

"Just with a kiss."

He lifted a hand from the water, and used it to tip her chin back so he could stare into her eyes. Much like he had when they'd kissed the day before, he leaned in ever so slowly, before softly pressing his lips to hers.

This time, as he kissed her, she felt a surge of power flooding through her, before settling near her heart.

Now, she was very much a Fae Queen.

TWENTY-ONE

Green was everywhere. All around her. Nothing but different shades of the same colour. Except that wasn't right. Soon splashes of other colours joined the greenness. There were pinks, blues, purples and yellows.

It was beautiful, and powerful, and just a little bit addicting. This was what spring felt like. Never having felt her magic before, she'd had no idea that this is what it would feel like to channel it.

After a few more moments of just colour, things began to change, and the splashes morphed into butterflies flapping away on the imaginary wind.

Bringing forth the birth seemed to be surprisingly easy once she'd been able to access the magic. All she'd had to was place her hands on the stone and the magic had rushed through her, filling every corner of her mind.

And now it was flowing out of her again. Towards the

human world where it would herald the blooming of flowers, and the birth of new creatures.

Slowly, and a little disappointingly, the magic started to fade away. While she knew it had to happen, that didn't stop the sense of loss she was feeling. But then again, she'd be feeling exactly the same in another year's time, when she had to perform the Birth again. And every year up until her future daughter turned eighteen and would take over the role.

Tomorrow, she'd meet the autumn and summer Queens. She'd tried to get the winter Queen to visit too, but apparently she was sick. Which was concerning to say the least. Paranormals shouldn't get sick at all. Even if they were missing their magic like the winter royals were.

The magic of spring faded away, leaving Aledwen naked in the middle of her throne room and surrounded by people. Though she soon felt a soft robe being pressed around her shoulders. She leaned back into the giver, taking a deep breath and snuggling into his warmth. It was definitely one of the twins. Cyprus if she had to bet. She wasn't completely sure how she was able to tell them apart. They were completely identical. And yet she definitely knew which one of them was which.

"Thank you," she said, only receiving a nod in return. Definitely Cyprus then. He only seemed to talk when they were alone, or just with her other mates.

"The Birth is complete," the Master of Ceremonies called out, and the fae around them cheered. Most likely because another party was about to begin.

Aledwen almost rolled her eyes. All the partying

really wasn't her thing. If given the option, she'd rather just retire to the library and talk with her mates. Especially as there were other, important things for them to deal with.

"Have you heard anything from your brother?" she asked Fane, once she was sure there wasn't anyone left listening.

"Not yet, but it's only been a day. I suspect we'll hear from him in another two or three."

"When he notices the magic is gone?" she clarified.

"Yes. I'm not sure how he even holds it, or how often he checks on it. I can't say I've ever tried to steal magic before," he replied.

"No, me neither."

Fane chuckled. "And let's hope we don't have to deal with bound magic again."

"We better not," Drey replied. "Besides, you may have bigger issues to deal with." He looked in Brandon's direction, and the shifter tried to look innocent, but failed miserably.

"What did you do?" Aledwen asked, slightly exasperated.

"How do you feel about family dinner?"

EPILOGUE

While it was nice not to be royal for a while, Aledwen was more nervous than ever as she waited outside the smart looking house with the twins on either side of her. Both Drey and Fane had wisely decided to stay back at the palace. Throwing in the fact that Aledwen was in a relationship with not just their sons, but two other men too, would likely be too much. Particularly for people that had a hard time accepting their daughter was with a bear shifter.

Brandon rapped smartly on the door, before opening it anyway and walking in.

"That's always been our family way," Cyprus said when he saw the confused look on her face.

"Alright then."

"You ready?" he asked, slipping his hand into hers and giving it a squeeze.

"As I'll ever be."

She didn't want to admit it, especially as she knew it

was really important to them. But she was nervous. She'd never had to meet the parents before. Mostly because she'd never been in any kind of relationship. Just had a few fun nights.

The decor was modern, but timeless, and she wasn't surprised to see photos of the twins and their two sisters adorning the walls. Apparently, the eldest wouldn't be here today. She was busy doing something with her children. Aledwen liked that. Family should always come first.

"Aledwen, right?" A redhead that looked a lot like the twins greeted her warmly, and it took her a little longer than she'd have liked to recognise the woman as Arabella. Even if they had been introduced once before. Cyprus and Brandon gave their sister a quick kiss on the cheek, before disappearing further into the house, leaving the two women alone. Most likely on purpose.

"Yes."

"It's lovely to meet you properly. I see you've managed to tame my brothers."

"I wouldn't go that far."

Arabella laughed lightly. "I'm not sure, I haven't seen Cyprus this relaxed in years. He couldn't stop talking about you the other day."

A blush rose on Aledwen's cheeks. She knew exactly what that compliment meant. Especially as Brandon had told her Arabella was the only person Cyprus had actually talked to. Before her anyway. The thought of which just filled her with pride.

The other woman began to lead her down the hall, past a photo of what must have been the Reed parents.

"Arabella..."

"Hmm? Call me Ari," she corrected her. "Everyone else does, it's just easier."

"Ari, do your parents know about our...situation?" She grasped at words, not quite knowing how to describe what she had with her men. They really should make a term for it. Then again, maybe they had in fiction.

"I don't think so. They know Cyprus is bringing someone, but I don't think they've ever twigged that he and Brandon have done the sharing thing."

"So they've done it before?" Aledwen's curiosity was piqued, and she longed to know more. Though this was probably something she should be hearing from the twins and not their sister. Maybe.

"Yes, though it went a little wrong, hence why Cyprus is...well, Cyprus."

"I'm sure they'll tell me one day," Aledwen said diplomatically, hoping it would convey to Ari that she wasn't going to pry until the men were ready for her to.

"Oh they definitely will. But there'll be a lot for you to learn now. They told me one of your other mates is a dragon? That's going to be a lot of new skills."

"What do you mean?" She was slightly alarmed. What new skills could the other woman possibly be talking about.

"Shifting?"

"I'm not a shifter."

"Not yet, no." Ari laughed a little, but not unkindly.

More in a couldn't-believe-no-one-had-said-anything way. "If you're mated to three shifters, then you'll gain shifting powers. And I must say, I'm fascinated to see how that one turns out. Will you just be a fox or just a dragon? Or some weird dragon-fox hybrid? Oh the possibilities!"

"A dragox?" Aledwen asked, bewildered.

"If that's what you're going to turn out to be, we're definitely coming up with a better name for it," Ari said, giggling slightly, and infecting Aledwen with the same joyousness.

"Oh definitely, that's a rubbish name. But it sounds better than fogan."

"You're right, I'll have to give you that one."

The two women entered the dining room, still both giggling away.

"Mum, Dad, this is Aledwen. Aledwen, this is my Mum, Diana, and my Dad, George."

Aledwen thought it was a little odd that it was Ari introducing the her to them, and not one of the twins, but she went with it. Maybe this was their way of easing them all into the multiple mates thing.

Dinner went surprisingly well, unless she counted the surreptitious touches the twins kept giving her under the table. Whoever had decided to seat them on either side of her, hadn't taken into account that the two of them would do just about anything they weren't supposed to.

Even so, it was making her smile. That, and the fact her men were right. She and Ari really did get on well.

She was impressed by the female shifter's intelligence, and the fact she held such a high position politically.

"Have you ever thought of trying for a position on the High Council?" Aledwen asked before taking a bite of the delicious dessert Diana Reed had made.

"Yes, but I don't think it's for me. A lot of shifters still need me, and I don't think I could abandon them."

"Not yet, anyway," her mate, Bjorn, added with a smile. "Just wait another few years and she'll have changed her mind."

"Bjorn," she scolded, but the adoring look on her face said everything. There was a lot of love between the two of them. Aledwen wondered if it was just as obvious between her and the twins.

No. Not love. None of them had used the word yet, and she wasn't sure she was actually ready yet. Soon though. Definitely soon.

"So, what is it you do, Aledwen?" George Reed asked, and she almost choked on her mouthful.

"I'm a fae Queen."

"And what is that, dear? Some kind of performer?" Diana asked.

"Mum!" Brandon protested.

"No, it's being the Queen of the fae. The Spring Fae to be precise." Aledwen took another bite of pudding, hating the way this conversation was going.

"But you're so young."

"Yes, there was an unfortunate set of circumstances that led to my coronation."

Both of the older Reeds looked a little skeptical, but

she was fine with that. They'd soon learn she wasn't joking. Probably around the time their future grandchildren were born, and they came to the palace to celebrate.

"Where did you meet Cyprus?" Diana changed the subject.

"At one of the balls," Aledwen answered.

"Oh."

"I'm going to clear the dishes. Brandon, want to help?" Ari half-asked, half-demanded, before jumping to her feet and starting to collect the dishes.

"Sure." He got to his feet and leaned towards Aledwen, giving her a kiss on the cheek. Her eyes half-closed, and a satisfied smile crossed her face. She definitely liked her men's affectionate sides.

"What is going on here?" Diana demanded, her voice stern, and kind of a little scary.

"We're clearing the dishes," Ari pointed out dryly.

"She's Cyprus' mate." The woman sounded outraged, and Aledwen had to remind herself to breathe so as not to lose it herself.

"I'm both of their mates," she said softly instead.

"That can't be possible."

"Why not?" Aledwen asked. "I certainly feel the bond as strongly with Brandon as I do with Cyprus, and vice versa."

"Because it's wrong."

"Why is it wrong? If they feel it for me, and I for them, then it's nothing but right." She could feel her magic rising up inside her, but had to squash it down again. Losing it now definitely wouldn't be good. After all, she'd only just gained it full stop. She certainly didn't have any control of it.

"It...I...it...."

"Let's just go, Dwen," Brandon suggested, gesturing to his brother.

"I-"

"No, don't bother," Brandon told her, just as Cyprus slipped his hand back into hers. He always knew just the way to do that which would offer her comfort. "Mum, Dad, I know this may be hard for you, but it's the truth. Aledwen is both of our mates, and we're both happy with that. You know where we are when you can accept that."

Aledwen watched the assembled family's faces, surprised to see remorse flicker over George's face so quickly. Less surprisingly, Ari and Bjorn looked equal parts amused and proud. It was Diana that concerned her. There was a clear look of disgust on her face.

Better not tell her what she'd been up to with her twin sons then.

"Thank you for a lovely dinner," Aledwen said graciously. "I hope to see you again soon." Hopefully with a little more understanding about the relationship she was part of.

"Please, Dwen, let's go."

The twins all but dragged her out of the house, before both turning to face her.

"We're sorry," Cyprus said. "I didn't think they'd be quite that bad."

"Me neither," Brandon added. "Please don't think we're like that." Their eyes both pleaded with her to understand, and her heart went out to them. How could she not understand. She felt the truth of their words as much as she heard them.

"I know. So long as we have each other, it'll all be fine."

"Very much so," Cyprus said, leaning forward and kissing her chastely, before pulling back so Brandon could do the same.

"It'll all work out in the end," Brandon added once he'd pulled away.

Yes. It would. Even with all the challenges ahead of them, Aledwen knew it would all work out. She had her men by her side after all.

The End

But worry not! This isn't the end of Aledwen's story. There'll be two more books of her coming later in the year! You can sign up here to get an email when the next Fated Seasons stories release. But until then, why not try Fated Seasons: Winter, starting with Saving Eira.

AUTHOR'S NOTE

Thank you for reading *Chasing Aledwen*, I hope you enjoyed it! As I mentioned in my dedication, I really want to thank my readers for this one. I messed up pretty big (hence releasing in February and not in January like originally planned), and yet you not only stuck by me, but supported me.

I also need to thank Skye MacKinnon, Kelly Stock/Bea Paige, Arizona Tape and Gina Wynn. You guys have made an unbelievable difference to my writing journey, and I really do feel far less helpless knowing I have you guys to help and support me...and to write with, let's not forget that!

So, a note on Fated Seasons! This is a twelve book reverse harem series, split into four. By season believe it or not! *Chasing Aledwen* is the first book of Fated Seasons:

Spring, with two more to come. Fated Seasons: Winter has also started, with *Saving Eira*, with the second and third winter books coming soon!

You can sign up here to get updates on Fated Seasons books and side stories (but just those linked to the Seasons!):
http://www.authorlauragreenwood.co.uk/p/fated-seasons.html

(p.s. If you're intrigued about the Reed twins' sister, Arabella, you want to check out The Vixen's Bark)

Laura is a USA Today Bestselling author of paranormal romance, and a lot of other stuff, including fairy tales, fantasy, contemporary and reverse harem. She can't decide on much!

When she's not writing, or doing authory things, you'll find her reading, cooking or baking...more or less successfully.

You'll also discover that she is a massive fan of random facts, and will talk about them for ages if you let her...so maybe don't.

Stalk Links:

Facebook Page:
http://facebook.com/authorlauragreenwood
Facebook Group:
http://facebook.com/groups/theparanormalcouncil
Bookbub: https://www.bookbub.com/authors/laura-greenwood

Website/Mailing List:
http://www.authorlauragreenwood.co.uk
Instagram: https://www.instagram.com/lauramg1406/

Listing all my books takes ages, and I won't subject you to that!
So I'll just be listing the first in series!

Other Paranormal Reverse Harem

Fated Seasons: Winter > http://books2read.com/SavingEira

Ashryn Barker > http://books2read.com/ShatteredIllusions

Seven Wardens (co-written with Skye MacKinnon) >
http://books2read.com/fromthedeeps

For more reverse harem titles:
http://www.authorlauragreenwood.co.uk/p/reverse-
harem.html

Other Paranormal Titles

The Paranormal Council >
http://books2read.com/thedryadspawprint

Thornheart Coven: http://books2read.com/witchspotion

Beyond the Curse: http://books2read.com/awakening1

Twins Souls (co-written with Arizona Tape):
http://books2read.com/soulswap

For more books:
http://www.authorlauragreenwood.co.uk/p/fantasy.html

And if you've read all mine...

Why not try some of my friends' paranormal & urban fantasy
titles...

Gina Wynn

Ho Ho Hocus > http://books2read.com/hohohocus

The Virgin's Destiny >
https://books2read.com/virginsdestiny/

Kelly Stock/Bea Paige

Sisters of Hex: Accacia >
http://books2read.com/accaciascurse

The Soul Guide > http://books2read.com/thesoulguide

Skye MacKinnon

Daughter of Winter > http://books2read.com/winterprincess

The Drowning > http://books2read.com/polardestiny

Ruined Hearts > http://books2read.com/heartoftime

Arizona Tape

My Own Human > http://books2read.com/myownhuman

Triple Threat > http://books2read.com/dannysdance

My Winter Wolf > http://books2read.com/wolfswhisper

Printed in Great Britain
by Amazon